CHANGING FATE

By Michelle Merrill

This book is for Regan, Sara, Christina, Ali, Brandon, and anyone else affected by cystic fibrosis.

May they find a cure soon so we can all breathe easy.

We are all human beings, but if we don't learn to *be*, we can never *become*.

Chapter 1

I reach into my backpack and wrap my fingers around my pill box, but I can't seem to pull it out. Maybe I'm a little embarrassed about taking meds with every meal...or maybe it's the girl with the blue-streaked hair who's staring at me across the cafeteria. She steps toward me. I grip the container and flip the lid open.

The girl moves closer and I reach my other hand in, dumping the pills into my palm. It's like a race, like she's trying to get to me before I put them in my mouth. Each step she takes makes my heart pound stronger against my ribs. But why would she care about my pills?

Maybe she doesn't. Maybe she's checking out a hot guy behind me and I'm just paranoid because I'm the new girl. I'll never understand why Mom thought it would be better to move during my senior year rather than wait six more months. It's true we're closer to the hospital now, but we were managing. Okay, so the last hospital run was a bit tense. Mom was so flustered she ran a red light, cut off too many people on the highway, and almost got into a serious accident with a minivan.

1

If she thought *that* was tense, the look the blue-haired girl is giving me would make her stomach burst with ulcers.

My insides scream for food and it feels like something is clawing its way through the empty space. I throw the pills into my mouth and wash them down. The blue-haired girl is closer now and I purse my lips, hoping she'll leave.

She doesn't. Instead, she comes right up to my table and pulls out the blue chair next to me. The feet screech across the floor.

"What you got there?" she asks.

"Nothing."

Her dark eyes focus on my hand. "Doesn't look like nothing."

I shrug. "What's it to you?"

Her mouth lifts on one side, revealing a protruding tooth. "You're the new girl, right?"

"First day."

"Well, then you don't know that all meds are supposed to be checked through the office first."

They were. Nurse Molly knows all about me. But I choose to keep that a secret. "I'm eighteen. What does it matter?"

She lets out a short laugh and takes in my small frame, everything from my skinny arms down to my little feet. "They don't care how old you are. It's the rules."

My eyes scrunch into a glare. "And what are you? The meds monitor?"

She crouches in the chair and leans closer. "Tell ya what. I won't say a word if you promise to share them with me."

2

I flinch, definitely not expecting that offer. Not that enzymes would do much for her. With all my trips to the hospital, I'm not sure they're doing much for me either. But why would she want them? Black market? Addiction? I shake my head. "Sorry. Not for trade. Go tattle if you want."

A look of disappointment crosses her face, but soon enough the protruding tooth is back. "Well, nice to meet you…"

I stare at her, thinking of other words besides *nice* to describe this conversation. I could tell her my name's Kate, but instead I say, "We didn't meet and I don't care to know your name."

She snickers. "You might want it when you ask me to return your backpack."

Someone yanks my backpack and the strap is suddenly out of reach. I drop my water bottle and jump up in time to see a boy swing a right down the hallway. I only hesitate a moment before taking off after him. A high-pitched laugh echoes behind me and hundreds of eyes follow me out the door. In the hall, I turn right and weave my way through the towering crowd. Down at the other end, the blond-haired kid is stopped at the next hallway with my purple backpack in his grasp. He looks back, probably watching for me.

Instead of charging my way through, I match my steps with the guy in front of me and use him to move closer. Suddenly, he stops and I lean away to avoid smashing into his back.

"Since when do you have a purple backpack, Charlie?" the guy asks.

The boy spins around and hides my backpack behind him. "What do you want, Kyler?"

3

"Who is it this time?"

Charlie shakes his head and I can't wait any longer. If I don't get my backpack soon, I'll miss lunch altogether. When I step to the side, Charlie's face falls and he backs up, ready to take off again. This time I'm right on his tail. The sudden exercise will come with consequences but I don't have time to mess around. I never thought I'd have to use karate in school, especially this soon. Mom barely lets me practice at home anymore. But I have no choice. In less than a minute I trip him, pin him to the ground, and tear my backpack from his hands.

"What the—" He tries to push me off.

I give him a flat smile and jump back to my feet. Passing a surprised Kyler, I hurry to devour the lunch my stomach wanted ten minutes ago. Forget that: my body has been aching for food all morning despite Mom's hearty breakfast of bacon and eggs.

Before I reach the cafeteria, a cough rushes up my throat. I try to suppress it and pick up my pace to get to my water bottle. A sputtering feeling tugs at my chest and I can't hold it back any longer. Air rips its way out my throat and I enter the cafeteria with my face buried in the crook of my arm.

When I glance at my table, my arm drops and I freeze. The girl is gone, my water bottle is empty, and my lunch is nowhere in sight. The clawing in my stomach collides with my anger and I clench my hands until my nails pinch my palms. I swallow my next cough and it backfires through my nose. Gross. Seriously. I grab a tissue from my back pocket and wipe my face.

Someone taps my shoulder and the tissue becomes nothing but a squished ball in my fist as I turn around. A girl

4

with a blanket of dark hair looks me in the eye. She may be an inch taller than me, but she couldn't be more than five-foot-one.

"Here," she says, out of breath, offering a sack lunch.

I fold my arms. "What's that?" After the chase I just finished, I'm not about to trust *anyone*.

"It's food. Vivian has a way of welcoming people to our high school."

"And you are?"

The girl smiles. "I'm Giana. Vivian has the blue hair. She thinks she owns this school and obviously thinks stealing food is the way to show it."

"Is she poor or something?"

Giana shakes her head. "Trust me, she's got money. I know it and I've only been here a few weeks."

"Wait. You're new? What grade are you in?"

She laughs. "I'm a junior, but most people ask me if I sneaked away from Kindergarten."

I nod, only because I've been in her place. "It doesn't get any better when you're a senior."

"Dang." She snaps her fingers. "I was really hoping they'd at least call me a first grader."

"Thanks." I reach forward and take the food.

"No problem. Kyler told me what happened."

I tilt my head and try to put a face to the familiar name.

"He says Vivian picked the wrong person to steal from."

He must've been the guy who seemed so surprised when I tackled Charlie. That's all I remember about him, though. Class is about to start and I need food. "I have to eat," I tell her. "Thanks for the help…and the food."

"Anytime."

Giana walks away and I sit at the nearest table. In no time, the food is out of the bag and on its way to my stomach. It satisfies my hunger but leaves me wondering why Giana was so nice. She doesn't even know me.

I'd already decided before moving here that I wasn't going to make friends. Because the moment I make friends, they usually find out about my cystic fibrosis. And once they find out their friend has a fatal disease, they might decide to run. It's happened before. It could definitely happen again. Besides, there's no way around it. No cure. One day, it will win the constant fight.

When that day comes, I don't want to leave people behind. That's why Giana and I will never become friends.

Chapter 2

Getting ready for school the second day is almost worse than getting ready for the first. This time I'll recognize people. They might remember my name and they might want to talk—which means they'll expect me to respond.

Before school starts, I slide my black percussion vest over my clothes and click the three straps across my stomach. It's similar to a life jacket with a tube connected to each side. The tubes are attached to a compressor that pumps air through the vest when I turn the switch. It pounds my lungs to keep the mucus from gathering, therefore preventing infections...most of the time.

During my night routine, I do homework to pass the time in therapy. Mornings are all about distraction. See, I dream a lot about different things that could go wrong with my disease and I need something to chase those thoughts away. The beautiful architecture and designs of famous buildings in France fill my mind. I close my eyes and daydream that I'm there: running my hand along the walls of The Palace of Versailles, or standing at the bottom of the Eiffel Tower, staring up at the intricate placement of support beams and cross bars.

What I'd give to visit France before I die. If only I could walk through the streets and drown out my fears with the soft language.

I move my hand across the desk until my fingers curl around a dart. Thinking of France calms me. Throwing darts releases anger. Anger at life. Anger at the disease that's killing me. Anger because there's no cure. Even though I can't imagine my life without CF, I wonder what it'd be like to eat a meal without medicine or look forward to my fortieth birthday party. Forty is supposed to be "over the hill." My hill has been reached and I'm already barreling down the other side.

My eyes fly open to the target across the room. I pull back my hand and force all the anger toward my fist and into the dart. It soars across the room and lands right where I aimed it, on the outer ring. It's more fun to hit the spot I want than to aim at the center of the target every time.

When therapy's over, my head and lungs are clear. I dash down the stairs for breakfast and try to fake a front jab to my mom's jaw. She catches my fist and twists it behind my back. If there's one thing to remember, it's not to attack your instructor. Mom earned her black belt five times, which is why they had her teaching the class by the time I came along. She always tells me that if Dad ever comes back, I'm free to take him down.

I try to imagine it but Mom snaps her fingers in front of my face. "Hurry and eat. You're going to be late."

She hands me my morning pills: vitamins, antibiotics, and enzymes. Sometimes there's more, sometimes less. It depends on what the doc thinks I need. Swallowing pills used to be hard, but now it's as easy as breathing.

I eat a quick breakfast, twist my blonde hair into a braid, and hurry out the door.

By the time I get to school, I'm so distracted by trying *not* to make friends that the sound of my name startles me.

"Your name's Kate, right?"

I turn in my chair and find a somewhat familiar curly-haired guy looking at me. His name escapes me until he sticks out his hand and says, "I'm Kyler." He moves his hand closer. "I think I ran into you yesterday."

I nod, remembering those freckles surrounding a pair of wide eyes. "You look familiar, but I don't think it's *you* I ran into."

Kyler laughs and his melodic voice washes over me, bringing back daydreams of French people talking to each other in smooth, connected tones. I hold my breath and wait for him to talk again.

"You're right," he says. "I think I can say that's a good thing. I'm sure Charlie will never come near you again."

I manage a small laugh and say, "Good." It kills me to have to respond in my boring, clipped voice. His words make my insides sway, like I've just stepped into an ancient chateau.

Kyler's hand drops and pats his leg instead. It wasn't like I was trying to be rude, I just wasn't trying to be nice either. Niceness leads to hanging out and connecting with each other. As much as his voice affects me, I know I need to stay *far* away. My gaze falls to his mouth and I notice a freckle on the upper part of his lip, just off-center.

The teacher walks in and I close my eyes. If anyone catches me staring at a guy's lips, it isn't going to be the teacher…or the guy. I promise myself right then that I'll never look at that freckle. It sends my mind into dangerous territory that has to do with kisses and feelings and—I can't think about that. It means I might make an attachment. Sure, he's hot. But I can't let it happen.

The teacher clears his throat and I face forward, keeping my attention on the board and my head in reality. Not that school will help much if I'm going to die, but Mom keeps reminding me that the average life expectancy for someone with CF is now somewhere around thirty-eight. And no, I'm not allowed to live with her until then.

I try not to think of leaving Mom, whether because I move out or something worse. She's all I've ever had, really. And even though it might be promising to make more friends, I still don't think I'll be able to create any kind of connection that could wither if they find out about my disease.

The hands on the clock tick and the teacher's voice drags on. With five minutes left, I pack my bag and have everything ready to leave right when the bell rings. Kyler won't have time to think about talking to me, let alone walking with me down the hall. My plan runs smoothly until I'm in my chair for statistics and Kyler walks in. At first I think he's stalking me, but then he sits down across the room and waves.

I lift my hand in a limp greeting and rest my head on my desk. How did I miss his face in all my classes yesterday? Did he just show up at lunch?

"Are you sick?" a male voice asks.

I consider avoiding the person, but if I'm going to pretend to punch him, I need a clear image of his face. I turn to look as a boy sits next to me, his hair is disheveled and his fingers are tight around a crinkled schedule.

10

"Hi," I say, hoping to satisfy his need to disturb my obvious misery.

"I'm new."

Really? How many new kids could there be? No wonder Vivian has a full time job making life miserable for the newbies. I think about warning him, but decide it might be more fun to watch, and even more enjoyable to ruin Vivian's plans. I even consider thanking him. He just gave me something to look forward to.

His soft skin and boyish eyes make me wonder about his age. "Are you a senior?"

He blushes. "No."

"Right. Some kind of math prodigy then."

His pink cheeks turn a deep red. "I'm a freshman."

A freshman about to get a lesson in new kid bullying. The teacher calls for attention and I point forward. "Looks like class is starting."

He shoves his schedule into his backpack and pulls out a tattered notebook.

Lunchtime can't come soon enough.

* * *

When I enter the cafeteria, Vivian is already at a table in the corner. Muted sunlight lights up half the room, leaving her in a shadow. The smell of gravy drifts up my nose and triggers a deep growl in my stomach. I hurry to find an empty table with a good view of Vivian and her posse. A few other kids surround her, mostly younger boys. Her eyes flick to my face and she leans back with a smug look, folding her arms across her stomach. I match her flaming glare with a cool gaze. The *tssss* of a sizzle echoes through my head.

11

The new boy walks in and I regret not learning his name. It would've been nice to know the name of the kid I might save. I still haven't decided what to do about that yet. Vivian gets out of her chair and nods to the boys at her table. They stand up together and approach the new kid.

Definitely not what I expected. Maybe it's a different form of initiation than the one they put me through. A minute into their conversation, the new boy's gaze switches to me for a brief moment. He shakes his head and turns back. I'm not sure if that's a good thing or bad. And why is he even looking at me? Are they talking about me?

Ooh, if I had a dart in my hand right now, I could use Vivian's blue streaks for target practice. My stomach growls and I quickly swallow my pills before Vivian attempts another "share your drugs" trick. I still don't know what she meant by that. Did she really want my pills or did she just want my food?

The group breaks up as I take my first bite. The boys fan out around the cafeteria and it's hard to keep my eye on them all. Vivian sits down at her table with the new boy and leads a lengthy conversation that includes batting lashes. When her arms start waving, her chest shakes—which is probably her intention. Whatever she's trying to make him do, her words aren't convincing enough.

I turn away to check on Vivian's minions. One, two, three, four...I can't find the fifth. Instead, Giana walks in and waves at me. I lift my head in acknowledgement and continue my search for the last boy. Charlie. Where in the world did he go?

I take another bite and find his reflection in the window. He's approaching me from behind, probably to steal my backpack again. In three seconds he'll be at my right shoulder and I'll show him what an elbow feels like.

Just then, Vivian stands up and huffs out a frustrated sigh. She throws her hands in the air and stalks away from the new boy. He glances at me with a smile that fades in a split second. Charlie grabs my backpack and I curse Vivian for the distraction. This time, I wait an extra minute to plan my revenge. The first time was—okay, I admit it—kind of funny in a little kid way. But I'm not a kid anymore, and there's definitely no humor the second time around. What are they trying to do, anyway? My lunch is half gone and my pills won't do them any good.

I stand up in time to see Giana chase Charlie through the side door with the new kid on her heels. I wonder how everyone got so caught up in this stupid charade. I grab my water bottle and plan my next move. If they've gone out the side door, they could be halfway around the building. I leave through the front entrance and cut across the commons. Then I work my way back and listen for footsteps.

Sure enough, sneakers slap the linoleum floor and I stick my head around the corner to see Charlie charging right toward me. It almost makes me sad that I don't even need my skills to stop him. All I have to do is stick my foot out. He stumbles over my toe and flies through the air. Mid-flight, I grab my backpack from his hands. It jars his fall and he crashes on the ground beside me.

He rolls to his back but I trap him with my foot on his chest and point my water bottle at his face. "What are you doing? Does it make you feel good to act like a little punk?" His face pales and his mouth moves but no words come out. I shake my head. "If you're going to act like a child, I'm going

13

to treat you like one." I open my water bottle and splash the last bit over his head.

Giana comes down the hall with new boy next to her. She's smiling like she knew I could handle it all along. The new boy snaps his gaping mouth closed and applauds. Right then, I feel bad for Charlie. He's on the floor sopping wet, not because he wants to be, but because he's friends with Vivian. I toss the water bottle in a nearby trash can and reach down to help him up.

"If I were you," I tell him, "I'd find some new friends."

He wipes away the water dripping down his face and looks at me. "How about you?"

For some reason I glance at Giana. She lifts an eyebrow and waits for my answer. This is it. The time when everyone in the school finds out that I want to be a loner. Better sooner than later. "No. Sorry. You wouldn't want to be my friend. You think a little water is bad? I can think of something worse. See ya."

As I walk away, the weight of loneliness settles on my shoulders. Great. As if I don't have enough to bother me. First I have to focus on avoiding people and now I have to feel selfish for doing it. If only they knew it was for them, not me.

I don't care much about dying. At least…I don't think I do. Sometimes I almost wish it were already here. But it's not. And even though I might be prepared for it, no one else will be. If I die, they'll be the ones without me, trying to overcome the loss. I can't do it to them. I watched my mom go through life like a broken marionette for too long after Dad left. No one deserves that, and I won't let anyone suffer because of me.

I continue down the hall and never look back to see Charlie's reaction.

Chapter 3

Mom comes in my room during therapy the next morning. She sits on the edge of my bed and eyes the dart in my hand, then glances at the large target across the room.

"Well, let's see it."

My lip rises on one side. I pull my hand back and throw the dart at the center of the target. It hits its mark and Mom's eyebrow arches.

"Still the best," she says. "How are you?"

I shrug.

"I just got a call from the doc. He wants to do some antibiotic treatments through the nebulizer. You know, to prevent winter colds and all."

A sigh escapes and I nod. I'm actually surprised he didn't order it earlier.

Mom stands up and walks to the door. "I'll pick up the new meds after work and you can do your first treatment tonight." She pauses and folds her arms. "I don't want to bother you about this so soon, but how are things at school with the other kids?"

I try to fake a smile but she just narrows her eyes and purses her lips. It's the usual sign that she knows I'm about to lie and she'll see right through it. "I don't have a lot of friends yet, but maybe by the end of the week..." Or never.

She exhales. "Please don't push people away like you did at your last school. You *need* friends. They'll help you see the happy things in life."

She's one to talk. Her only friends were in the karate group back home. "I *am* happy, Mom. I have you and I have my hobbies."

"As much as I love you, honey, there's more to life than hanging out with your mom and throwing darts."

"You're right." I say. "I *do* need people. I need them to build awesome structures that I can admire from far away. Maybe one day I'll get to live in a palace. I'd love to see the Eiffel Tower, you know."

"Yes, yes. I know. Maybe you can find some rich friends to pay for the trip."

I laugh. "That's so wrong, Mom, and you know it."

"But it might help you make friends even if they don't use their money to buy your happiness."

I pick up a dart and aim it at her. "Goodbye, Mom. I'll see you when I'm ready for breakfast."

She swipes her hand through the air with wicked speed and leaves the room. *Show off.* She'd totally do it too—knock the dart out of the air if I tried to hit her with it.

I think about Mom's suggestion through the rest of morning therapy. By the time I walk into my first period class, I still have it on my mind. I either have to actually make friends or find a way to lie about it so Mom doesn't keep pestering me. I find my seat and notice that Kyler's not there yet. The bell's about to ring and he might be late. Or absent. Not like I should care.

17

I don't.

A melodic voice drifts from the corner behind me. My stomach dances in smooth motions. Warmth seeps through my body and leaves a tingle on the back of my neck. I turn around to find Kyler talking with the teacher. They shake hands and Kyler pivots around, catching my eye before I can look away. Dang. Heat races to my face and my heart pounds erratically.

That's when I notice the teacher looking back and forth between the two of us. He says something to Kyler that I don't understand because everything around me is a haze of embarrassment. Kyler walks toward me and a sliver of panic spreads through my body. Most likely, he's going to tell me to stop staring and to take a picture of him because it would last longer. Or maybe he'll tell me to leave him alone, which would be perfectly fine since that's my goal anyway. Right? It's my goal. No friends. I repeat it in my head until he stops beside me.

"Hey, Kate. Good to see you."

I nod with, I'm sure, a ridiculous, dumbfounded look. "You too." I close my eyes and try to get a grip on reality. Maybe he'll just walk on by. Even though his voice fills me with a strange hope, he has that freckle on his lip that I refuse to look at. My eyes pop open and I find it. Right there. And he's speaking to me again.

"There's an assembly in a few minutes. I've gotta go because I'm in it, but I'll catch ya later?"

Is that a question? Like he's asking my permission to speak to me again? Maybe my star struck look didn't scare him...yet. I clear my throat. "Yeah, sure. Good luck with whatever you're doing in the assembly."

Kyler's smile almost has the same effect as his voice. He leaves the room and turns down the hall. A few minutes later, we file toward the auditorium. Before I find a seat, Giana appears and pulls me by the arm. We head toward the stage, moving closer to a group of people calling her name. Lots of people, together, like a bundle of friends that are connected in a way I can only imagine. I yank my arm back and Giana stops. "Don't you want to sit with us?"

I gnaw my lip and consider the consequences. Friends, connections, death, loneliness. My hands are suddenly clammy and my legs tremble. I shake my head. "Sorry, but I'd rather sit alone."

"You sure?"

I'm just glad she's not pushing it. "Yeah. Thanks though."

The back of the auditorium is empty and inviting. I find a seat next to the aisle. Students shuffle by, talking to each other and racing to sit next to their friends. A group of guys walk past and when they're gone, Giana's standing right beside me. It's like she keeps appearing out of nowhere. I guess that's a bonus for being short in a crowded school.

She waves. "Can I sit next to you?"

I stand up and plop in the next seat. "What about your friends?"

She shrugs. "They'll live. Besides, I don't like being so close to the stage. The loud noise drives me crazy."

"Really?" Does she mean it or is she just trying to make an excuse to ditch her friends and sit next to me?

"Yeah, I'm part deaf in one ear and even though it makes things quieter, it also makes everything kind of echo through my brain. I get a headache when it's loud."

19

"From the noise?" I ask.

"I'm not sure. It could be that my ear strains to pick up specific sounds. Who knows?"

I shift in my seat. It's weird listening to someone else's problems instead of focusing on my own. "Were you born with it?"

Giana shakes her head. "No, I got in a car accident when I was little. The doctors say I'm lucky to be alive. From what they can tell, after all the surgeries and recovery, the only permanent damage was a loss of hearing and maybe a little stunted growth."

"A little?"

She laughs. "When you see my parents, you'll know what I mean."

When I see them? Like, she's already planning on us meeting sometime. I swallow and can't think of anything else to say. I don't want her to think I'd like to meet her parents, so I close my mouth and look forward.

A few minutes later, the red curtain on the stage parts and a girl steps through with a microphone in one hand. Music plays through the speakers and she lifts the microphone to sing a soft melody. The volume grows and grows until another voice joins her. This one I recognize. It melts my heart and covers my skin with goose bumps. Kyler is here, but not on the stage. The students turn in their seats, searching the crowd for him. Fingers point and faces light up, all of them looking my way.

I spin around and find Kyler walking across the back of the auditorium; he comes down the side, passing right by us. My heart beats hard, pounding like it wants to fly out of my body and latch onto the words that float from his lips. The tune is slow and sung in a different language. It's not French, but it might as well be with the way he sings it. Just when I think he won't notice me, his head turns mid-note and a smile spreads across his face. I curl my fingers around the end of the armrest and hold on tight. No one in my whole life has ever looked at me that way. Of all the crushes I've had, Kyler is the first to ever make me feel like my dying insides are still alive.

When the song ends, I hold onto his lingering words, letting my heart throb, my stomach flip, and my hands tremble. Kyler jogs to the stage to join his choir group and they perform a boring ballad together. But his gaze lingered long enough. I don't think my heart will ever work correctly again. So much for it being the only thing I can rely on to keep me alive.

Mom's advice echoes through my head. She told me friends would help me see the happy things in life. As much as I don't want her to be right, she might be. My whole life I've wanted to be alone because I didn't want to hurt anyone else. But there are things I might be missing out on. Like Kyler singing to me, making my pulse spin. Normally, I would've avoided the whole assembly, or at least tuned out to listen to my ipod. I would've missed his smile, his soothing song. But instead, I'm content, maybe even a little bit happy.

A knot forms in my stomach. I stare at the kid's head in front of me. Even If I want people in my life, I've spent so much time trying to be alone, I'm not sure I can learn to let them in.

The assembly is a blur. Kyler doesn't perform any more solos. Once it's over, Giana turns to me. Her eyes are bright and her grin is contagious. "I have a great idea."

"Better than chasing Charlie down the hall?" It's not going to be a normal day here without an encounter with Vivian and her gang. Charlie probably won't try to steal my backpack again either. Yeah, definitely going to miss that.

Giana snaps, "Are you listening?"

I lift an eyebrow. "Yes?"

"There's a party this weekend and you have to come."

I shake my head out of habit.

She holds up a hand. "You don't have to tell me right now. Think about it and give me your answer when you sit next to me at lunch."

I purse my lips and wonder how she got so good at manipulating people. No, I don't want to go to a party. And no, I don't want to sit next to her at lunch. A nagging feeling in my stomach reminds me of my earlier self-doubt. I've never been to a party but I'd be lying if I said there wasn't a small part of me that wants to go.

Giana stands up and I make a sudden decision. Before I have time to think my way out of it, I grab her arm with shaky fingers and pull her back down. "I'll go."

She tilts her head. "Are you sure you don't want to think about it? If you don't want to go, it's okay."

Don't think don't think don't think don't think. "Yes." The word tumbles out and I almost sigh in relief. "I'll go. Tell me the time and place and I'll be there."

"You want a ride?" she asks.

A ride. A friend. A connection. Maybe this is how to let people in. I bite my lip and nod.

"Great." She whips out a pen and paper from her purse. "Write your address here and I'll swing by around eight on Friday."

22

The pen trembles in my grasp, but I squeeze it tight and write down my new address. Mom will be so pleased, and hopefully I will too. This may end up worse than Vivian sabotaging my first day of school, but all I can do is hope for the best. It's the same thing I go through every night when I close my eyes.

Hope for the best and prepare for the worst.

Chapter 4

Mom didn't have time to get my meds, so we head to the store Wednesday evening. Nothing exciting happened at school. Not that I can expect much since I try so hard to have it that way. My psychology teacher talked about fathers. Father-son relationships. Father-daughter relationships. At least I can say I don't have one of those.

"How was school?" Mom asks.

I shrug. Maybe I look like my dad.

"Are there any cool kids in your classes?"

Another shrug. Or maybe I sound like him. How weird would that be?

"Did you sit by anyone special?"

I barely hear her question. My hair might match Dad's. It's been a while since I've looked at his picture. Kind of hard to do when it's hidden under my bathroom sink.

"Kate."

I blink and turn to face Mom.

"What's on your mind?" She flicks the turn lever and we enter the parking lot to the local grocery store. The asphalt is wet from the afternoon storm, the looming clouds hovering low. We wait as an elderly lady shuffles toward her car.

I wonder why Dad really left. Mom hates talking about it, but sixteen years is a long time to wait for answers. "Were you and Dad having problems before I was diagnosed with CF?"

Her fingers tighten around the steering wheel. "I thought we'd talked about this."

"No," I say, cautiously. "Every time I want details, you change the subject."

She parks the car and turns off the ignition. Her gaze pierces the windshield. "Marriage is hard, Kate."

I groan, sick of vague responses. "Even harder with Dad?"

"He was in his final months of residency. Life was stressful. Besides, we never saw each other. He barely knew you."

"I was two years old. He had to know me a little."

She runs a hand through her hair. "He spent more time in the hospital than with either one of us."

"So...he didn't leave just because of my diagnosis?"

Mom finally looks at me, her expression hard. "He said it was the last straw."

Or just the best excuse to bail out of personal responsibilities. "You'd think he'd understand more since he *is* a doctor."

"That's just the problem. He understood too well." Mom takes a deep breath. "It scared him."

He could deal with the problems at work but he couldn't deal with them at home. Maybe he felt like work would never end. He'd leave patients at the hospital just to come home to a permanent one. That's all I was to him. Another patient. So he left. No custody battle. He gave Mom

25

everything she wanted, except a husband. He didn't want anything to do with me, just gave up his parental rights and walked out the door. Mom refused child support so every link between us was severed.

"We're doing okay, right?" Mom asked.

I still remember when Dad stopped by eight years ago. As much as I hated him, part of me wanted to see him. But I never did. "Sure, Mom," I say, my voice flat. "Everything's great."

She nudges my chin with her fist. "Let's pick up your prescription and get something yummy for dinner."

I force a smile and get out of the car.

After we pay for my bag of meds, Mom leads us past canned foods and cooking ingredients. When we reach the aisle containing every random necessity, she stops in front of the nylons and picks up a nude pair.

"Since when do you wear those?" I ask.

"Since my boss moved me up to office manager."

I grab her arm. "Really? But you just started working there."

Mom laughs. "They needed someone right away."

"What happened to the previous guy?" Not that I'm complaining. My mom could use the steady income. It's better than karate lessons and part time accounting work.

She exchanges the pantyhose for a darker pair. "Apparently he thought the company's money was good enough to fund his upcoming cruise."

I lean back. "No."

"Not to mention the last few trips with his wife and three kids."

How convenient. "Good thing he got caught. And even

26

better that they picked you for the job."

Mom's gaze lands on a pair of tan nylons. I grab the nude color that matches her skin and toss it into the cart.

"You sure?" she asks.

"Unless you want to look like you only tan your legs. It's up to you."

She pushes the cart a few steps and grabs some bronzer makeup. "I could make my face match."

I take the bronzer and put it back. "You don't want to scare everyone."

"If I wanted to do that, I'd just wear some of this." She rubs her finger on a lipstick sample and applies the dark purple color.

"That's gross. Do you know how many germs you just spread on your lips?"

"Probably not half as many as you're touching on that cart."

I grimace and reach into my bag for a sanitizing wipe. Before I open the packet, I rub my finger on the bright pink lip sample. "Here, Mom." She lifts her head and I smear it on her cheek.

Her eyebrows reach high. "Now you're asking for it."

I step away and tear open the wipe package with a laugh. "Wouldn't want to get me sick, would you?"

Mom leans toward the lip colors and I unfold the wipe in record time. She digs into a crimson red and comes at me.

I catch her by the wrist. "Mom."

"It's a good color, Kate." She pauses and looks at her finger.

"Red?"

We laugh so hard, I snort. Somewhere between my

hysteria and trying to get a wipe out for Mom, I catch sight of curly brown hair. Freckles. Coming my way. I toss the wipe to Mom and duck behind the cart so Kyler won't be able to see me.

"What are you doing?" Mom asks. "I didn't even get any on you. You look fine."

"Shh." He can't see me—not with my Mom. Not with anyone. As much as I want to hear his voice, I don't know what to say.

Mom glances over her shoulder and turns back slowly. Her lip curls up on one side. "Someone you know?"

"Can he see me?"

She checks again. "Hurry. Pretend like you're looking at something on the bottom shelf."

I reach for a bouncy ball as Mom walks off with the cart...leaving Kyler standing three feet away. He's holding two cans of shaving cream, studying the front of each. I could try to run before he notices me, catch up with my mom. She probably thought this was a good chance to trick me into making friends. I put the bouncy ball back on the shelf and turn to leave.

"Kate?"

I pause for a second then remember how much I like his voice. I turn around with a smile. "Hey. I didn't even see you."

"Yeah, it's like you came out of nowhere."

My cheeks burn and I try to clear my throat. "Probably because I'm short."

"That's not a bad thing. Sometimes I wish I could hide that easily."

I want to ask him from what, but it's not the right

28

time…and he probably wouldn't tell me anyway. He doesn't even know me. "So, grocery shopping, huh?"

"Yeah. My dad's here somewhere."

I lean my weight on one hip. "My mom just disappeared."

He chuckles and my heart goes into overtime. "Funny how they do that," he says. "I have to find him soon, though. I've got voice lessons in a little bit."

"No wonder you're so good at singing." I bite my lip. He isn't supposed to know I'm thinking that.

"Thanks." He reaches in his pocket and pulls out a folded piece of paper. "Dang. I forgot I had the grocery list. Dad's probably lost."

"You always come shopping together?"

He looks to the side and the paper crinkles in his grip.

Maybe I said the wrong thing. He might hate the fact that he's shopping with his dad. I need to say something to erase the crease in his forehead—something that will keep him talking. "How long have you been in singing lessons?"

His shoulders relax. "Only a few months."

"That's great." Except my voice doesn't sound like it's great. It's hollow and forced. I've isolated myself for so long now, I'm not exactly sure how to respond, or what else to talk about.

"How long have you been fighting?" Kyler asks.

I tilt my head. Fighting? "Oh, karate."

He nods and his curly hair springs up and down.

"I took lessons when I was younger but I don't do it much anymore."

"Could've fooled me."

I chuckle. I'm not sure I even used a real move on

29

Charlie when I took him down. It was instinct, like a ravenous monkey.

"I'm surprised Vivian actually told him to steal your backpack again," Kyler says.

I raise an eyebrow. "He didn't *have* to listen to her."

Kyler's lip pulls up on one side. "Charlie's just adventurous. And he likes getting chased by girls."

A man with short brown hair approaches Kyler from behind and stops. His eyes are familiar.

I say, "I think your dad's here."

Kyler spins around and the man lifts his chin in greeting. "You left me with those chickens," he says in a low voice. "I didn't know which one to choose."

Kyler throws the list in the cart. "It was good to see you, Kate. I better get going."

"Sure."

As Kyler walks away, I hear him say, "Come on, Pops. Let's go sort out those hens."

I grab the bright red lipstick and scan the aisles to find Mom. Not only does she owe me a yummy dinner, but with a stunt like that, she's going to get one back. The lipstick will go great with her new nylons.

Chapter 5

I see Kyler at school a couple times the next day, but he doesn't pay much attention to me. Every time I hear his voice, I strain my ears to listen. The soft tones run together like smooth cream. I close my eyes and feel the hope of a brighter future take me down the streets of Paris where I can enjoy a cool drink and admire the arches of the Sainte-Chapelle.

Yes, now those thoughts usually include him. It's hard not to think of him next to me, teaching me the history of French art, or something about their culture. Every time I open my eyes, though, he's busy with different things—meaning real friends and super awesome hobbies that don't involve me. I wish I could sing, but no amount of wishing could change my monotonous voice. Another trait I inherited from my mom.

My new nebulizer meds seem to help me breathe a little better. Still, Mom constantly reminds me to wash my hands, use tissues when I can, and sanitize…everything. It's second nature to me, but maybe she doesn't understand that. Or maybe she's just worried. I think she worries almost as much as I do. She's the only person in my life, and since my grandparents passed away, I'm the only one in hers.

Things are slow at lunch with Vivian. Apparently, her streak of bullying the new kids came to an abrupt end after Max, the math whiz. After he refused to help Vivian get back at me, he spent the rest of the week assuring me that he wasn't even tempted to join her group.

By Friday, I can't stand to hear his Vivian story anymore. He sits next to me in statistics and starts a conversation just like every other day.

"How's it goin', Kate?"

I force myself to acknowledge his greeting with a nod of my head and a dart in my mind. "It's fine." And will continue to be fine if he doesn't bring up Vivian again.

"Do you know of any new kids coming soon?"

I clench my hands and think of several karate moves that could make him shut up. After a deep breath and an imaginary karate session, I offer a fake smile. "Contrary to what you may think, Max, I don't sneak into the office to find out when a new kid is coming. I just happened to meet you the day after I moved in. I knew Vivian was going to bother you, so I waited. I didn't expect her to ask for your help and I didn't think you'd be so quick to refuse."

He flinches. "You thought I'd help her get back at you?"

I scream in my head and fight a sudden urge to glare at him. "No. I didn't even think she was smart enough to come up with a plan like that. Honestly, anyone who has to bully to feel better about themselves has much bigger problems."

"So…what you're saying is that Vivian has some personal problems."

By this point there's no hiding my annoyance. My face feels flushed and I consider leaving class. "I don't care what problems she has. And I don't care what she's planning next. In fact, I'd like to never hear her name again."

Max stares at me like he doesn't know what else to talk about. I clench my fists and let my gaze wander. The teacher approaches Kyler and they have a quick conversation. I'd give my best darts to know what they're saying. When they finish, Kyler stands up, walks toward me, and turns to face Max.

"The teacher wants us to switch seats."

Max leans back and I can see the panic in his eyes. "Why?"

"He needs you to help those kids over there," he says, pointing across the room.

Max grins and I know Kyler has said the right thing. Whether that's what the teacher really wanted or not, Max believes it and seems pleased. He grabs his stuff and turns to me. "I'll see ya around, Kate. If this guy bothers you, let me know." He takes a few steps and pauses. "And if you ever need help with your math, I'm always available."

I wave him away with an encouraging smile. My shoulders fall and I hunch over my desk.

"That bad, huh?"

I rub my temples and let Kyler's voice soothe away some of the anger. "You have no idea. Remind me to stay away from the cafeteria whenever there's a new student."

Kyler laughs and I breathe a little easier. "Just can't help yourself," he says. "You have to save the day if given the chance."

I sit up and face him. "It's not about saving anything. It's about showing bullies you don't need to push people around to be tough."

"Vivian will never forget that now, thanks to you."

"Oh, I'm sure she's over it. Luckily, I don't think Charlie is. She might have to find a replacement. And no, Max won't do it. She already tried. Too bad."

"You want him to help her?"

I look into his eyes and suppress the urge to glance at his lips. "I don't want anyone to help her. I'd love for him to leave me alone though."

Kyler tilts his head and taps his pencil on the desktop. I want him to say something, to listen to him talk and know what's going on in his head. Suddenly I wonder why the teacher hasn't started class. The surrounding voices mix together and Kyler's gaze starts to make me sweat.

Finally, he says, "You seem to want everyone to leave you alone."

A knot forms in my throat. Why would he say that? His words are deep, and thoughtful, and rub me the wrong way. Of all the people I've pushed away, it's never been him—which means he's noticed my actions and might think he'll be shoved aside as well. As much as I love knowing that he pays attention, it also makes me nervous to think about what might come next. Does he want me to let him in, to be friends and to make a connection? A shiver shoots up my spine as I think of the jump it'll take to get over my emotional wall.

Even though I've started to climb that wall with Giana, I'm not sure I'm ready for more yet. But I should be. I mean, it's Kyler, his voice alone is worth the jump.

Before I can say anything, the teacher finally starts class and I look at Kyler one last time. Our eyes lock and I just hope my eyes say the things I can't get my tongue to speak. Like how much I want to smash that wall just to know I might mean something to him. He stares back and the air between us becomes charged with something that wakes up the life within me. Fluttering wings rush through my stomach while my heart stomps each beat. It's so hard to breathe; I think for a second that maybe my CF has taken over my lungs.

When Kyler looks away, I fill my chest with air. My insides settle down but a burning feeling continues to creep up my neck, seeping into my face. I close my eyes and inhale slowly. As much as I want to push this feeling away, I'm afraid if I do, I'll never feel it again.

* * *

I look for Giana at lunch, but she's not there. We've eaten at the same table for the last few days and she's been more than happy to let Max sit with us. I'm beginning to think she's happy about everything. Max might not ever get on her nerves, but I wait for him to find a different seat before I sit down at a table of my own. I reach into my backpack and grab my pill box.

"Can I sit next to you?"

I drop the box and straighten up to find Kyler ready to sit in the chair beside me. A knot forms in my throat, trapping my air. I glance at my backpack as my mouth turns dry. "Sure," I say.

He pulls a lunch from his backpack and sets it on the speckled table. "We never finished our conversation earlier. I was going to ask if you're going to the party tonight."

He's going too? First he finds me in the crowd at the assembly, then he sits at my table, and now he wants to know if I'm going to the party? This might be too much, too fast. I'm not sure I can handle being around so many unfamiliar

35

faces. It's hard enough thinking about it. Maybe I could fake a sickness. "Are you sure it's the same one?"

"Giana said she invited you."

"Where is she?" I ask, hoping to change the topic.

"At the dentist."

I think I remember her telling me about that. I guess I forgot it was today.

"Aren't you going to eat?" Kyler asks, taking another bite of his sandwich.

I stare at my food and try not to think about the consequences of skipping the enzymes with a meal. Maybe it won't be so bad. The effects shouldn't hit until long after the party tonight anyway. But is it worth keeping my CF a secret? If I'm going to make friends, they need to know *me*. All of me and all of my problems. They need to know what they're getting into so they can decide to back out like Dad did.

But I don't want Kyler to back away. Not yet. A curl bounces over his forehead and I crunch my teeth into my apple. Hopefully if I don't eat too much, it won't be so bad.

A few of Kyler's friends join our table: an Asian boy with a plaid shirt and a blond kid in a wheelchair.

"Kate, this is David and Vic."

I lift my hand in greeting.

"Guys," he says. "Kate."

"I like your hair," Vic says.

A blush spreads across my cheeks. "Thanks." My gaze settles on his wheelchair for a brief moment. Of course, I'm curious if he's had it his whole life or if it's a temporary thing. Either way, it's not something he can hide. And Kyler accepts him as a friend. I should just take my pills and tell him, but the thought makes me cringe. Maybe one day. Just not *this* day.

36

I focus on my food and listen to their conversation. They're talking about soccer players, or maybe basketball. Some kind of sport with goals and balls. Could be football. Since I can't follow, I pretend I'm sitting in a cathedral, the organ music calming my soul while my eyes memorize each piece of stained glass. That is where I belong: with my own thoughts in my own head.

* * *

After school I watch a documentary about French artisans while doing my nebulizer meds. Usually when I eat carbs without enzymes, my stomach aches a few days later, but my stomach has been seeking revenge all afternoon. I spent the better part of my last class in the bathroom and I seriously considered going home.

Once I'm done breathing through the tube, I switch that machine out for my percussion vest. The therapy helps settle my stomach a little, but Mom can still tell there's something wrong at dinner.

"Don't you have a party tonight?" she asks.

I swallow my pills and nod.

She puts her fork down with a frown. "Please don't tell me you agreed to go just to make me happy."

"No. I really want to go, I just don't feel well."

Mom's stern look falls and the familiar worry lines crease her forehead. "Is it an infection?"

I shake my head. As much as I don't want to tell her about skipping my enzymes, she's going to drill me until it comes out anyway. "I didn't take my meds with lunch."

She purses her lips and waits for an explanation.

37

I press my hands to the table and wait an extra second. "Someone sat next to me at lunch and I didn't want to explain it to him."

Mom's face turns a shade of red. "Him? Kate. This is your life. I thought you were okay with it."

"I am. I just don't want other people to push me away."

"*You're* the one who's pushing."

My legs tremble and I clear my throat to stop the rising lump. "I'm trying not to. But it's hard to get past the fact that they still might not accept me for who I am."

Mom sighs. "They won't do that."

"But they might."

Mom pinches the bridge of her nose. "If someone has a problem with the real you, they're not worth having around. You have to stop thinking everyone will be like your dad. He wasn't worth it."

"Then how did you ever have me?"

Mom's hand drops and her eyes narrow on mine. "Everyone makes mistakes. That was one of mine. Don't punish yourself for my problems." She stops a beat, her eyes glisten. "*Please*, don't hide the real you. People can be accepting but you have to give them a chance."

First she wants me to make friends and now she wants me to just lay my personal secrets out on the table for them to judge me with? The churning in my stomach gets worse and my appetite disappears. I stand up and walk around the table to kiss my mom on the head.

"Aren't you going to eat?" she asks.

"No. I've got a party to get ready for."

Chapter 6

Giana shows up a little after eight o' clock. I give Mom a quick hug and follow Giana to her four door sedan. The front bumper is dented and the red, chipped paint is faded along the edges.

"It's not anything special," Giana says as I settle into the passenger seat. "But it gets me from one place to another."

I run my hands along my jeans. It took me almost an hour to decide what to wear. And it took me another hour to braid my hair loosely over one shoulder and add a touch of makeup. Applying mascara is so much harder with shaky hands. For some reason, I want to look just right. It might have something to do with Kyler being at the party. Or maybe I don't want to appear frumpy, tired, and worn out.

Unfortunately, I think it's both reasons.

"You okay?" Giana asks.

I swallow at nothing and clear my throat. A slight pain pinches my stomach and bubbles gurgle through me. "I think so."

"You don't look so good."

Of course. Even when I try hard, it still doesn't help much.

"I mean," Giana says quickly. "It's not that you look bad, you just don't seem excited to go tonight."

I shrug, not knowing how to respond. Excited wouldn't be the right word. I'm looking forward to it, but between my upset stomach and fear of making friends, I'm still reluctant about the whole thing. "What kind of party is this anyway? Will there be drinking? Dancing? How about movies and games?"

Giana gives a short laugh. "Maybe a little of each. But we're not the rowdy type. Usually if there's alcohol, it's because someone spiked the drink to be funny. I'm not sure what Tammy has planned for tonight."

"Do I know her?" I try to recall Giana's friends, but none of them come to mind.

"She's the skinny, tall one who wears too much makeup and flirts with everyone."

And…that didn't help me at all. Almost everyone is taller than me, wears more makeup, and flirts like normal conversation won't ever capture a guy's attention. "Maybe you can just point her out when we get there."

"Which will be in a few seconds. Here's her house."

Giana pulls the car behind a line of vehicles and a rush of fear makes my pulse race. I open the car door and step onto the sidewalk to straighten my corduroy jacket. Giana leads the way to the front door and I glance back at the car, wondering if I could hide inside before someone notices I'm even here. I shake my head and clench my fists. I can do this. It's nothing worse than facing any doctor with bad news. A bad infection should scare me worse than a group of teens.

Without knocking, we walk into the house. A leather couch sits against the far wall in the front room with a grand piano in the middle. It's too empty, quiet. I'd always imagined parties with pumping music, people talking, and lots of bodies that you have to push to get anywhere.

"Tammy?" Giana calls.

"We're back here."

We pass through the entry and walk by the kitchen to a family room tucked in the corner of the house. A bay window juts out the back and Kyler sits in front of it. The room smells like popcorn and I find the bowl being passed around as guys and girls fill their plastic cups.

My stomach growls and I check my pocket for my enzymes. They're gone—stuck in the pocket of my last pair of pants. Missing a dose with one meal isn't too bad, but twice in one day? Not good. I press my hand to my stomach as we move to the edge of the room. Kyler scoots over and pats the ground. "Come sit here," he says to us.

A dark-haired girl with high cheekbones and bright red lipstick trails her fingers down the arm of the boy next to her. She pats his hand with a giggle and turns to wave us in. "Now we can start," she says. *That* must be Tammy.

Giana turns to me with a smile. "I told Tammy I'd help her out tonight so I'm going to sit close in case she needs anything. You want to sit by me or Kyler?"

There's definitely not enough space by Tammy for the two of us. "I'll sit by Kyler," I tell her. On my way over, I try to avoid everyone's gaze, focusing on the empty spot of beige carpet next to him. I kneel beside him and he moves closer. Suddenly, the room feels crowded. Heat radiates off my skin and I'm sure my face is as red as Tammy's lips. I inhale and think of France. I imagine people sitting on their balconies, sipping their nightcaps and laughing, in casual conversation. It

41

soothes the noise around me and calms the raging storm in my stomach. Mostly. More bubbles dance through my body and I hope they don't plan on escaping anytime soon.

Talk about embarrassing.

"How about a game of truth or dare?" Tammy asks.

A few girls clap their hands and I try to catch Giana's eyes. I thought she said this wasn't going to be *that* type of party. She finally looks over at me and nods her head.

"Not tonight," she says. "Any other ideas?"

"Spin the bottle." I turn to find a girl that looks a lot like Vivian with pink hair.

"That's so old," someone else calls out.

"What about just truth?" Kyler says. "Dares are stupid anyway."

If he didn't smell so yummy and sound so nice, I might have given him a cross punch to the nose just for the suggestion. Truth means that people will find out more about me. Truth means discovering secrets that are meant to stay hidden. Truth means opening up and connecting. I clench my teeth and hope that someone else has a better idea.

The silent room kills that hope.

Giana shrugs and I take that as her consent. She snaps her fingers and points to Tammy who stands up and shimmies her tight skirt down a little further. If the guys didn't have their eyes on her before, they do now.

"Here's how it'll work. The person on your right will ask you a question and after you answer, you ask the person on your left something you're dying to know."

"And what if someone refuses to answer?" pink-haired girl calls out.

"Just lie about it and move on," Kyler says.

42

He bumps fists with the guy on his other side and Tammy rolls her eyes. "No lying. Since we aren't playing truth or dare, we'll just say that if you don't answer, you have to kiss someone in the room."

More fist bumps—even the girls join in this time. No one's going to answer any questions now.

Tammy giggles and tells everyone to settle down. "I'll go first."

I try to pay attention to her question and even more to the answer from the boy beside her, but I don't want to know anything about these people. Knowing things will make me care about them. Instead, I listen halfway and let my mind wander. Different words and phrases catch my attention, but they don't stick. One boy gets up, crosses the floor, and plants a kiss on the mouth of a red-headed woman. I say "woman" because she's got more chest than I could ever dream of. And she looks older, like she's already in college. Her flushed cheeks and wet lips tell me that she liked the kiss.

The boy goes back to his seat, next to Kyler, and I tune back in. What if Kyler doesn't answer his question? Who's he going to kiss? I lick my lips and taste a faint strawberry sweetness from my leftover lip gloss.

"Kyler, why don't you drink?"

The room goes still. I think up to this point, the questions have been light and silly. This one weighs down the mood and gets everyone's attention. Kyler stares at the floor, his thumbs twirling in circles as he bounces a leg. His mind is somewhere else. I know that look. I get it every time I think about something important: life, death, my dad leaving, my mom suffering.

I don't want to know his answer. If it causes that kind of reaction, it can't be good. Kyler snaps out of it. He smiles, turns to me, and lifts a hand to my face.

I freeze. My lips part and my eyes focus on the single freckle spotting his upper lip. My next breath catches in my chest and I wait for him to close the distance. His thumb caresses my cheek and he exhales a soft, minty breath across my chin. My hands tremble under my weight and I lean forward.

The moment seems to last forever.

And then someone says, "Seriously? You just want some new girl action."

Kyler's face goes tight. He leans back and drops his hand. The moment is ruined. "Who says I don't drink?" he asks.

I blink a few times and close my mouth. What was that? Was he really going to kiss me? The guy who asked the question hits Kyler on the shoulder. "Go take a sip of that punch on the table then."

"Jack spiked it."

"Hah! See. You don't drink. Now I want to know why."

Kyler grips the guy's shoulder and chuckles. "Because someone has to take care of all you losers when *you* do."

The guy shrugs out of Kyler's reach and ends his turn.

Before Kyler can see the frozen shock on my face, I turn away and gulp down some air. I won't look at him. How can I? He was about to kiss me but he didn't—like I'm not good enough. Not that I really want him to kiss me, it just would've been an interesting first kiss. But his thumb was so

44

smooth on my skin. And his eyes roamed over my face like he was memorizing each angle.

"Kate."

I lift my head and stare at the crown molding. Kyler leans closer but I refuse to look at him. His breath moves the loose hairs around my face and I slam my protective barrier into place. No emotions, no connections.

"Do you ever think about dying?"

The question lingers in the air. At first I think it might've been in my head, but all eyes are on me now. They wait for my response and I have to force myself to think of the question: the one thing that's always on my mind. But if I admit that I do, then they might ask me why. And that's something I won't admit to anyone, let alone a group of strangers.

I stare ahead like a deer trapped by the beam of multiple headlights. But which way do I turn? Which path will lead me to safety? Give them a quick yes or avoid the question and make the most of my first kiss? I glance at the guys in the room. Of course Kyler would be my top choice. But if I kiss him, I might not be able to stop. I turn to the boy on my left, lean close, and touch a light peck on his lips.

He pulls back and holds up a hand. "Whoa. What was that?"

A gasp from the other side of the room is followed by, "Vivian is going to flip."

I whip my head around to see the pink-haired Vivian look-alike gaping at me. I lean closer to Kyler and ask, "Who is that?"

Kyler's arm touches mine and I keep still. "That's Vivian's twin sister."

45

"And who did I just kiss?"

Kyler's mouth lifts on one side. "Vivian's had a crush on Jack for two years."

"Ugh." I grab the end of my sleeve and rub the life out of my lips.

"That bad?" Kyler asks.

"Where's the bathroom? I need to wash it off." And get away from all the sudden attention.

Kyler stifles a laugh and points to a door past the kitchen, toward the front of the house.

"Thanks." I stand up and flee to the bathroom. Once I make it inside, I lock the door and sink onto the toilet seat. Kyler was going to kiss me, but he didn't. Instead he asked me a question I didn't want to answer. And since I didn't want to give him what he denied me, I kissed some stranger who just *happened* to be connected with Vivian—blue-haired Vivian who has a twin with pink hair. I bet they had fun fighting over which colors they'd use.

Just as much fun as Vivian will have fighting over a boy I don't even want. There aren't enough darts in the world to keep her away from me. I know her wrath is coming.

I get up and wash my lips with the foamy hand soap. My stomach churns again and I think I'm going to be sick. Maybe Giana can take me home. Voices drift through the door and it sounds like the game is over. I walk out to find most of the group milling about the kitchen, stuffing chips and handfuls of candy in their mouths.

Jack stands next to the punch bowl and catches my attention with a crooked grin. He lifts his drink and winks at me. I spin around and make my way to the empty couch. As long as I can stay invisible, I shouldn't have to worry about making friends.

The leather couch is still warm from the last people who sat there. I lean into the stiff fabric and close my eyes.

"Are you germ free?" I blink my eyes open as Kyler sits next to me with a bottle of water in his hand.

"I hope so."

He rests his head against the cushion and stares across the room. I wait for him to say something more. His question made me think of dying and I need his voice to remind me that I'm still alive. That there's a place worth living for and his voice will take me there. "Sorry I asked that question," he says.

A knot forms in my stomach and pushes against the pain already there. I scramble for something to lighten the mood. "Maybe I wanted to kiss Jack."

Kyler lifts an eyebrow and looks sideways at me. "By your reaction, I doubt that very much."

I laugh. "Oh yeah? Why did you lie about your question?"

His eyebrows pinch together and he sits up straighter. "Lie? That was a half truth."

"You were obviously avoiding the real answer."

Kyler shrugs, killing the conversation with a sip of his water.

"Maybe you can answer me this," I say. "I know you take voice lessons but you haven't been in them very long. Where did you really learn how to sing?"

This time I know I'm not dreaming his faraway look. The plastic bottle crinkles under his grip and he looks at me with sad eyes. "My mom taught me."

47

"She must be a good singer then."

His gaze turns hazy and he whispers, "She was."

My body's sinking, falling into a memory that I thought I'd never live again. I'm ten-years-old and my mom's wandering around, checking each room for Dad even though he's been gone for eight years. There's a knock on the door and she answers. Her face falls. It's him. It has to be. Her hands clench into fists and she presses her lips into a thin line. He asks to see me, basically begs Mom to let him in. She holds up a hand to keep him out, tells him I died, and slams the door in his face. Tears stream down her cheeks and a light sob fills the room. There's another knock but she doesn't answer. Neither do I. He broke her heart once and I wouldn't let him do it again. I had to let go. I had to accept his first decision to run away.

He's dead to me.

But Kyler's mom really *is* gone. And now he carries part of her with him. I don't even know what to say. A dull feeling sinks in my chest. One thing's for certain: I won't be the one to make him suffer again. He can't get connected with someone who will smash his broken heart and leave him empty, searching for the right songs to soothe his grief.

Giana squeals. I crane my neck to see her lift her cell phone. "My sister just had her baby girl! I'm an aunt."

Girls giggle, boys clap, and Kyler and I just sit here.

Yay for her. And yay for everyone who will have babies. That's something I've never dreamed of because the chances of it happening are so slim.

I wrap my thoughts into a tight cocoon and wait for the party to end.

Chapter 7

Monday morning, there's a tickle in the back of my throat. I grab the bottle of water on my nightstand and guzzle for as long as I can take it—which, of course, is way too much. And now I'm coughing.

I crawl out of bed and strap on my percussion vest. When I reach for my darts, they aren't anywhere near me. They're sitting on the target where I left them yesterday, which means I'm stuck in this chair for twenty minutes with nothing but my mind to keep me busy. And that can be a dangerous thing. I close my eyes and find Kyler's face staring at me. His gaze is soft and a few curls fall across his temples. Freckles cover the bridge of his nose and sprinkle the rest of his face.

I shake my head like an etch-a-sketch to erase the image. It doesn't work. Now Kyler's eyes light up like he's seeing something he wants. What could it be? My heart flutters beneath the pounding air in the vest and my eyelids fly open. It's the only way to get him out of my head. I swallow a rising lump in my throat and take a deep breath. Since when did I have each part of Kyler's face memorized?

Beside the target on the opposite wall sits a picture of Notre Dame. I focus on the detailed arches, the twenty-eight chiseled statues of different kings, and picture myself at the top. One day I'll see it all. I'll conquer my disease, find a cure, and book a plane to France.

But not today. Today I get to go back to school and finish out my senior year one day at a time. The thought of sitting at lunch with Giana actually brightens my mood. And maybe seeing Kyler in real life will keep him out of my head.

* * *

On my way to psychology, Vivian emerges from a side hall and blocks my way.

"How dare you kiss my boyfriend," she whispers.

I blink once, my mind racing for a quick response. "If he's your boyfriend, why weren't you at the party with him?"

She flinches and her jaw shudders. "You wouldn't catch me dead at a party with Lily."

I open my mouth to ask who she's talking about—

"My sister was nice enough to tell me about your make out session."

Instead of words coming out, a laugh escapes. "Making out?" I can't even think of a comeback. The idea is so ridiculous. And the look on Vivian's face is priceless. No, I choose to do something far worse. "He's a great kisser. You should know."

Vivian presses her lips together and her face burns a bright red. Her mouth moves but no words come out. I consider walking away, but I'm more interested to see what she'll eventually come up with.

It takes almost a minute, but finally she says, "Well, when I make out with him, I'll be sure not to get him sick."

50

The joke is done. My stomach falls and panic presses down on my chest. "He's sick?"

"He hacked up a lung or two just this morning."

Normally, that phrase would've been a great description. But I'm not normal, and if I get a sickness like his, it might do serious damage to my lungs. My mouth turns dry and a sudden cough tickles the back of my throat. I hold it back and walk away from a satisfied Vivian.

"What?" she calls. "Can't handle a little cough?"

I need water. A drinking fountain calls my name and I race to it before the cough can escape. I sip the water and wonder why I'm even coughing. Is it because I'm worried about coughing or is it something else?

Unfortunately, only time will tell. Coughs are normal for me. They're part of cystic fibrosis. This is normal. I just need to repeat it in my head all day. Normal. Normal. Normal. I'm not getting a cold. Maybe Jack doesn't really have one either. Vivian's probably lying just to bother me.

I practically run into someone.

"Oh, Kate."

I step back to get out of Giana's face.

"I didn't see you," she says.

"Sorry. I was a little distracted."

Giana snags her lip with a tooth. "Yeah, me too."

That's when I forget my problem and wonder about hers. Her eyes are puffy and red. Her little nose looks like it's been rubbed too many times and her shoulders are hunched around a pile of books in her arms.

"Are you okay?"

It takes her a minute to answer. She pulls the books closer to her chest and says, "I think so."

51

"You sure?"

The bell rings and she stiffens. "I'll talk to you later. I don't want to be late."

She takes off down the hall before I can even say goodbye. I get to class right before the teacher calls attendance. Kyler turns around and his face matches the one in my memory. It's perfect. I mean, perfect as in I had all the details right. The teacher is already talking so Kyler just waves and faces forward, giving me a good view of his brown curls—which I stare at and have memorized by the end of class.

No wonder I don't know much about psychology. I spend most of my time in la-la land.

After class, I shove my notebook in my bag and catch Kyler before he's out of his seat. "What's up?" he asks.

I suppress a dreamy smile at the sound of his voice and try to focus on reality, not the images of Paris racing through my mind. "Do you know what's wrong with Giana?"

His eyebrows pull together. "What do you mean?"

I try to think of the best way to describe her troubled state. "She seemed sad this morning and I just hope she's okay."

Kyler checks the clock on the wall. "I'll see what I can find out and let you know in statistics."

I nod and he steps past me. His arm brushes mine, sending heat through my body. It calms my worries and keeps me distracted until I take my seat in our next class and wait for Kyler.

"Did you miss me?"

Max's voice snaps me back into focus. His boyish eyes are like a pleading cat's, large and glistening. I wonder if it's something he practices in the mirror. "Um…"

"It's okay. It's not like we were best friends or anything."

I lift my eyebrows and hold back the response at the front of my mind. He doesn't want to hear my opinion on our friendship, or rather the lack of one. "How's your—"

"Hey. I heard about your make out session with Jack. What a great way to get back at Vivian."

Wait. What? My jaw is hanging and all thoughts are paused. "What did you just say?"

"I said—"

"Oh, never mind." I suppress the urge to kick something. "I think I got it. How did you hear about that?"

He shrugs. "In the hall?"

Is that a question? Did he hear it in the hall or not? Ugh. What's wrong with everyone? Maybe it would've been better to deny the kiss in front of Vivian's face. Someone probably overheard and spread the word faster than a plague.

Kyler comes in the room and heads my way. He stops at his seat, staring down at Max. "How's it going?"

My eyes narrow on his face. "We were just catching up. Nice to see you, Max." I hold my breath and hope he gets the message. I need him out of here so Kyler can tell me what he discovered.

Max looks between us and Kyler offers a friendly smile.

"I'll catch ya later," Max says.

The second he's gone, I turn to Kyler. "So?"

He shakes his head slowly. "I asked a few of my friends, but no one's seen her."

"That's weird." I try to remember which class she has now but I can't get them straight.

"Maybe she went home."

It doesn't seem like her to skip school. Something has to be wrong.

"What's up with that kid?" Kyler points a thumb over his shoulder toward Max. "Does he have a crush on you?"

"Who knows." I rub my forehead. "Remind me never to kiss another guy."

He grimaces. "You kissed him?"

"No. Haven't you heard the rumor? I made out with Jack last Friday."

Kyler laughs and I want to smack the smirk off his face…but it might ruin those freckles so I fold my arms instead. "That was *some* kiss," he says.

I grimace. "Puh-lease." Not that I had anything to compare it to, but I knew it wasn't spectacular.

"I guess you've had better, huh?"

I tap my fingers on the desktop and glance at the teacher, wondering why he hasn't started class. I *need* him to start class so I don't have to answer Kyler's question. Maybe I should lie and tell him they've all been better. All zero. The specifics didn't matter.

Kyler's eyes focus on my face. "You've had others, right?"

And he just *had* to ask. I bite my lip and shake my head.

Kyler's eyes go wide. "Really? You're kidding me right?"

"No. Now stop gawking. It's just that…I've never had anyone to kiss." It's kind of a hard thing to do since I've never been a fan of making friends, let alone making out.

Kyler closes his mouth and looks away. He's probably hoping the teacher will start class right now so he doesn't have to respond. An awkward lull grows between us and I wait for him to say something. *Anything.* I don't want my plea of desperation to be the last thing on his mind.

He cracks his knuckles and puts his backpack on the floor. "I tell you what."

I raise my eyebrows.

"Jack's a lucky guy."

"Because he gets to be on the other end of Vivian's crush?"

Kyler grins and his freckles bunch together around his eyes. "No. Because he didn't deserve to be your first kiss."

My heart pounds against my chest like my percussion vest. It rattles my emotional wall and shoots heat to my face. I can't find my next breath, let alone a coherent response. My hands tremble as I reach into my backpack and pull out my statistics folder. Before the teacher can start class, I turn to Kyler and find his eyes on mine.

"Thanks," I say. He nods and an explosion crumbles the wall between us. How can I push him away when he treats me like I'm worth more than a broken down pancreas and a couple of worn out lungs? I feel like a statue brought to life, and Kyler has sung his way into my heart.

Chapter 8

Giana really did leave school, which makes me wonder what upset her so much. In order for me to avoid endless make out accusations with Jack, I eat lunch alone in an empty hallway. It's kind of nice to be away from Vivian's death radar, Max's attempts at conversation, and Kyler's map of freckles.

Okay, so that last part's not true. Just the thought of Kyler makes my pulse jump and my hands get clammy. But it isn't worth more stares and whispered gossip about the new girl kissing someone. It's like there's nothing else to talk about. I'm not even the new girl anymore; it's been a whole week. My head falls back against a metal locker. One week is still new...even for a pair of pants.

I eat my lunch, make it through the end of the school day, and finally have a moment to call Giana once I get home. But she doesn't answer.

By the next morning, I still haven't heard anything. That's not even the worst of it: the tickle at the back of my throat is now a constant bother. I cough my way through therapy, which makes dart throwing impossible. Then I cough my way through breakfast and Mom gives me a look over her fork full of eggs.

"Have you been using the nebulizer meds, Kate?"

I nod and swallow the food in my mouth. "I think there's a cold going around school."

Mom's eyes harden. "Then you're staying home."

It's not a bad idea. At least it would give a particular rumor time to settle down. But I really want to know what's up with Giana. And since she's not answering her phone, the only way to find out is to hope she makes an appearance at school today. "I promise to stay away from the sick kids."

"You'll have to wear a mask," Mom says.

I curse the dang mask and cough into the crook of my elbow. "How about I skip the mask but if I feel worse tomorrow, I'll stay home."

"And you'll stay away from anyone who even *looks* like they've got a cold?"

I think of Jack and the wildfire rumor. "Far, far away."

* * *

I don't see Giana before school starts. When I walk into first period, Kyler's there, standing by my desk like he's waiting to tell me something.

"What?" I walk quickly toward him. "Have you seen Giana?" I check my thoughts and wonder when I became so worried about someone other than myself. Even the sudden cough isn't bothering me much.

"Yes," Kyler says. "I don't think you need to worry, though. She seems fine today. Maybe a little down, but not as bad as you described her yesterday."

I sigh and a pinch of tension leaves my shoulders. "I wonder why she never returned my call."

57

"She's still a little quiet, which isn't like her. Maybe she's got something going on and just needs time to work it out." Kyler touches my arm and I freeze. Maybe if I don't move, he'll keep his hand there forever. "Sometimes life happens, but if anyone can see the good side, it's Giana."

Of course he's right. I've never seen Giana anything but happy—which is why her distress bothers me so much. When Kyler pulls his hand away, I want to tell him to stop—to leave it there and whisper nice things into my ear. Really, anything out of his mouth would be nice, especially if it's soft enough to be whispered. Kyler goes to his seat and I sink into my chair.

Kyler speaks so highly of Giana. Would anyone ever say that about me? Happy and eager to see the bright side? I've accepted my disease, I've even accepted death. But maybe there's more to it than that. Mom's always telling me that accepting something is more than just being resigned to the future. Giana has gone through terrible things. The accident she was in as a girl took away part of her hearing and almost killed her. She doesn't walk around with a chip on her shoulder like I do.

Maybe if I focus on the good, I'll be happier with my life. Knowing death could come anytime is one thing. Being okay with it is another.

Choosing to be happy in spite of it has never been easy.

* * *

Right when the lunch bell rings, I hurry to the cafeteria to find Giana. I'm halfway finished with my meal before she comes through the door, shuffling her feet and gazing at everything like she's stuck in a dream.

58

Kyler thinks this is better? Just because she's not crying doesn't mean she's happy. She's not even okay. I wave her over and she sinks into the seat beside me.

"Where did you go yesterday?" I ask, hoping it sounds casual enough.

A quiet sigh escapes her lips. "I'm sorry. My sister texted me with some bad news."

"Your sister who just had a baby?"

Giana's head moves up and down once.

"Is everything okay?" I lean on the edge of my chair and wait for her to tell me what it is.

She shrugs. "I think so. It's nothing serious yet. But it can turn into something very bad."

Story. Of. My. Life. I rack my brain to figure out Giana's vague puzzle. "Is it her or the baby?"

"It's the baby."

Ugh. She's killing me. Not literally, but I can see this isn't the time to get any real answers.

"Can I ask you something, Kate?"

I take a sip of water to finish my lunch. "Sure."

"Why didn't you answer the question at the party the other night?"

My hand tightens around the bottle. If I knew everyone was going to ask me about it anyway, I would've answered it the first time. At least then I wouldn't have to go through this over and over again. And the strange kid two tables from me wouldn't be puckering his lips in a mock kiss either.

Do I ever think about death? Definitely. Every night when I go to sleep. And every morning I think about life. They go hand in hand. But how am I going to focus on being happier? What's the key behind not thinking about death and

59

just focusing on real life every second of the day? That morning when I was so focused on Giana, I forgot about my problems. Maybe that's the key.

And maybe answering this question for Giana will help her with whatever it is she's going through. I set my water bottle down and look her in the eye. "I didn't answer because it's something I think about all the time. And it scares me."

Giana sits up straighter. "Really?"

I nod.

She lifts her hands and I can see a surge of emotion choking her. "Why?"

My pulse beats hard in my neck and I think of the best way to answer without telling too much. "It's going to happen to everyone eventually."

Tears pool in Giana's eyes and she swipes her cheek with her palm. She sniffs back more tears and as much as I don't want her to cry again, it's too late. She responds through her sadness. "I suppose some will face it earlier than others."

I stare at the tabletop and try not to think too hard about what she's saying. It's something that has been on my mind since I was old enough to understand the details of my disease.

Suddenly, she cries, "Oh, Ava."

I touch her shoulder. "Is that the baby's name?"

She nods and I find a tissue in my pocket to give her. She blows her nose and says, "My sister found out the other day that her baby has something called cystic fibrosis."

It's not possible. It's too rare. This can't be happening. My world is crashing. My heart is breaking. A thousand feelings burst within me and I can't hold them back any longer. I'm scared for the little girl, hate that there's no cure, and my heart aches when I think about her upcoming treatments and hospital visits—but somewhere in there I know she'll be okay. She'll have a special relationship with those closest to her.

The connection with my mom is one that I can never take for granted. I close my eyes and let her years of love bring me peace. Giana's niece will be okay. I am okay. One day there will be a cure and until then, the only thing we can do is help each other.

For that one reason, I open my eyes and wrap an arm around Giana. She shakes with a sob and I tell her, "It will be okay."

"But Mom said her great aunt had it too."

It makes sense since it's hereditary. Two recessive genes equal one terrible disease.

Giana hiccups. "And her great aunt died when she was two."

"That was a long time ago. Your niece will live longer."

"But what if she doesn't?"

So many what-ifs. That's the dark cloud around CF. No cure, just a bunch of hopeful dreams. But it's those dreams that keep us going, giving us something to look forward to— like climbing the stairs of the Eiffel Tower. I lick my lips and offer a weak smile. "They probably caught the disease early enough that there isn't any major damage done to her body yet. Now that they know she has it, they have lots of treatments and medicines that will help her. She could live to be in her late thirties. And if they find a cure, maybe she'll live longer than you."

"But is it enough?"

"It has to be," I say. "You can never give up on her. Not now, not ever."

After a silent minute, Giana's shoulders settle and she lifts her tear stained face. "How do you know so much about this disease?"

Deep breaths don't come. I settle for shallow ones that constrain my lungs. A sudden rhythm dances in my neck. Heat creeps across my skin in jagged paths. I squeeze my hands together until the stretched skin over my knuckles turns white. "Because." One deep breath, a head full of dizzy thoughts. I close my eyes and say, "I have CF too."

Giana's face falls and she finds more tears. It's too much for me. I can't breathe, can't think straight...can't sit and watch her grieve anymore over this. It's pulling me down, drowning me with fears I thought I had under control. I pat her arm and walk away.

Chapter 9

After my conversation with Giana, I take my mom's advice and go home. Not that my cough has grown any worse, but telling Giana about my disease makes it seem like I've shouted it to the whole world. She's not one to gossip, but I just feel so vulnerable. Like I've cut out my heart and revealed my deepest secret: the one thing that defines me, controls my body, and makes me so scared to die. And even more scared to live.

By the time I get home, I'm exhausted. I throw my backpack on the floor and lie on my bed, falling into a deep sleep.

Someone shakes me awake. I don't know what time it is, but it couldn't be much later. The smell of sweet flowers and coconut hovers over me. A groggy moan escapes from deep inside my body as I slowly lift my eyelids. Mom stares at me with panic. *Now* I'm awake. I sit up and she falls back, but stays close to me.

"Mom, what are you doing?"

"Me?" She runs a hand through her hair. "The school called to tell me you weren't in your last classes. Are you sick?"

Despite a sudden cough, I reassure her that I'm fine.

"Why did you come home?" she asks. "And why didn't you call me? I would've excused you."

I check the clock and see that Mom's home two hours early from work. "I'm sorry. I needed to rest and fell asleep before I could give you a call."

"Do you feel any better?"

"A little."

She exhales and the creases in her forehead disappear. "What about that cold?"

I shrug. "Might not be anything."

Mom pats my leg. "It's time for your therapy. I'll see you downstairs in a little while."

She gets up and I think about what her reaction could've been when the school called. Of course she would've prepared for the worst and hoped for the best. Hopefully she didn't really think the worst had come. "Mom," I say. She pauses and waits for me to talk again. "Thanks."

"For what?"

I sigh. This is me trying to be happier. To appreciate what I have and make life better for those around me. "For not getting mad that I left school. Sorry I scared you."

Mom comes back and kisses the top of my head. "Don't ever feel sorry. I'm just glad it wasn't something serious."

She leaves the room and I fill my nebulizer with the liquid meds. I hold the tube to my mouth and take a deep breath.

Twenty minutes later, I put my nebulizer away and reach for my percussion vest. I slip it over my shoulders, strap the front together, and turn the machine on.

I barely hear the knock at my door. By the time I realize what's going on, the door's already opening. I know it's not Mom. She wouldn't knock, especially since she knows I'm in the middle of therapy.

Dark hair comes around the door and Giana's eyes find me…in my vest, more exposed with my disease than I've ever been in front of anyone besides my mom. I grab the darts on my desk and throw one at the target. It misses the center ring, which I actually aimed for this time. What do I say to her? What will she think about all this? It doesn't matter what she thinks. She'll have to get used to it sooner or later. I throw another dart that hangs a left and wonder why Mom let her come in. She doesn't even know I've told anyone. She sure has a way of forcing me to make friends.

I grunt softly and let another dart release from my fingers. This one barely makes it on the target at all. Giana sits on the edge of my bed and crosses her legs. She's quiet, watching me, waiting for me to acknowledge that she's even in my room. I wrap my fingers around the rest of the darts and throw them all at once. Only one sticks. My head falls back in surrender and I turn to face her.

"Well?" I ask.

She smiles and I wonder how she's suddenly so happy. "How are you?"

I gesture to the vest and shrug. "Normal."

Her happiness fades. "I'm sorry."

I think I know what she's apologizing for, but I respond just to make conversation. "For what?"

"For not saying anything when you told me about your CF. For being such a spaz about the whole thing."

I run my finger along the ridges of the tube connecting my vest to the compression machine. "It's okay. Trust me. I've seen worse."

She laughs. "I doubt that."

That's because I haven't told her about my dad. "Well, you're here. Not only that, but you obviously got over it quickly."

"Thanks to you."

I tilt my head. "What do you mean?"

Giana uncrosses her legs and leans forward. "I thought my niece was going to die right away. I was so wrapped up in what might happen that I never stopped to think about the possibilities. My sister was no use and Mom's been MIA helping with the baby since she was born. But now I know she'll be fine. You're here and alive."

I shift in my chair. I'm fine. I'm alive. "It won't be easy for her all the time," I say. "And it won't be easy for your family."

Her eyebrows scrunch together. "What do you mean?"

"I'm fine *now*. But sometimes I'm not fine. Sometimes I have an infection so bad, I'm in the hospital for days. The disease may affect her pancreas, it may affect her lungs. Or she could be like me and it will affect both."

Giana rubs the back of her neck. "So what's the vest for?"

I point to the tubes. "The air pounds my chest and keeps the mucus out of my lungs to prevent infection."

"How often do you do it?"

"At least twice a day."

Giana closes her mouth, probably digesting the information. As nervous as I was to tell her about my disease, it gets easier every time I share something else—explain to her how I stay alive.

"How can you help your pancreas?" she asks.

I reach for my enzymes and lift the pill box so she can see it. "I have to take enzymes with each meal so my body can break down my food and help my system absorb the nutrients."

She sits back down and folds her arms. "What else?"

I shrug. "Extra vitamins, fiber, antibiotics. Sometimes I use a nebulizer and sometimes I use an inhaler. Everybody reacts differently to the disease, but the docs know what we need."

Giana stares at the carpet and bites her lip. After a minute she looks at me. "So...why can't someone with CF live a long life?"

I rack my brain for the best way to put it. "There are lots of things that can kill us. Since there isn't a cure, we just have to chase the symptoms away. But even with all the meds and treatments, we still get infections that do a little damage each time. We can only handle so much...eventually our bodies have to give in."

I thought it would be harder to explain, but this is something I've known long enough that it doesn't seem to bother me. At least, it never has before. She's quiet, so I try to explain further. "It's like hitting a spike against a rock every single day. No matter how many times you move the spike, it still does damage. And eventually, the rock will break."

Giana lifts her head with a determined look in her eyes. She jumps from the bed and snaps her fingers. "Then we'll just have to find a cure."

Just like that, she's decided to conquer the impossible. I can't help but smile. She'll never *really* find a cure, but I appreciate her enthusiasm. The alarm on my phone rings and I shut off the percussion vest. Mom comes in and avoids my gaze as she asks Giana to stay for dinner.

"No thanks. I have to get going, but I'll be back another time." She waves goodbye and slides past Mom.

I unstrap the vest and take a deep breath in. "Thanks, Mom."

She turns around. "Wow. What's happened to you? Here I thought I was going to get a double jab to my chin and you're thanking me. Did she already know?"

"Her new niece, Ava, is now a CFer."

Mom rubs her jaw and frowns. "Dang," she whispers. She pauses and I know what she's thinking: that this little girl has a hard life ahead of her. That she won't know any difference, but that she'll wish for something better every day. "That's really too bad." She looks at me. "Giana's lucky to have you, you know."

I shrug. No one's ever been called lucky to be in my life. If Giana does find a cure—if *anyone* finds a cure—I'll finally be the lucky one.

Chapter 10

On my way to class the next morning, I notice several students walking by with a small sheet of white paper in their hands. So many that I wonder why I don't have one yet. I stop and try to peek over a girl's shoulder as she reads the words. Unfortunately, she passes by too quickly. I move on, headed to my first period class.

When I turn the corner, I slam into someone. I step back, holding my nose. My other hand forms a fist and I look up to see whose face I'm going to punch. Jack. I flex my fingers to resist the sudden fighting urge and glance at his wild black hair and shiny red nose.

"Sorry—" cough, "about that—" more coughing, "Kate."

I step back again and move my hand down to cover my mouth. With the way he's coughing, the whole school will be sick. Why is he even here? If I didn't get sick from kissing him, breathing in his air will definitely seal the deal.

He glances at my nose.

"It's okay," I say. He leans closer with a questioning look. Shoot. He probably can't hear me. I back up to the wall and lean against it, putting three feet between us. My hand drops and I take a shallow breath. "I said it's okay."

"You sure?"

I point to my face. "No damage."

He wipes his nose with a tissue. "I'm afraid there's more I should apologize for."

"Like?"

He steps forward and I press my body into the wall. There's nowhere else to go unless I walk away completely. "I'm sorry about all the rumors. I didn't know Viv would be that mad. Someone must've told her it was more than a kiss."

A confession fills my mouth but I clamp my teeth together and smile. "It's fine." I want to change the subject, anything besides talking about that kiss. It was my fault. I kissed him and Vivian thinks we made out because of me. "Sorry about your cold."

"It's been coming for a while. Actually, it might be a sinus infection now."

I cringe. Infection? Not a word I like to hear. "I better go. Class is going to start soon."

Jack tries to say goodbye but it gets lost in a sneeze. Just hearing it makes my throat go dry. I swallow and try to suppress the urge to cough. It doesn't work. Now I'm coughing. Both of us. Jack eyes me and shakes his head. The rumored make out couple coughing, sharing each other's germs. There's no way to kill the stories now. I close my mouth and walk away.

Kyler's waiting in front of our psychology class, holding a small square of paper. I stop in front of him. "Can I see that?"

"Sure," he says in a way that shouldn't make my knees go weak, but it does.

He hands me the paper and the first thing I see are two letters. C and F. Really big. With the words cystic fibrosis underneath. My fingers tighten and the paper crinkles between them. I skim over the rest of the information covering the basics of the disease including the Cystic Fibrosis Foundation website and ways to donate to the cause. "Where did you get this?"

"Giana."

My mouth drops.

"She says it's good to be informed of these things."

I toss the paper back like it might burn me. "Did she say why?"

"Nope. She handed it to me on my way here."

The tardy bell rings and we find our seats. I can't help but notice Kyler glance back at me like there was another reason he'd waited to catch me before class. My heart beats a rapid pace, something like *Kyler's hot...Kyler's hot...Kyler's hot...*I can't breathe. He shouldn't have that effect on me. He faces forward and I try to focus on my dancing pulse, but another feeling is taking over.

It's something I can't place, but I know what it's from: the flyer. Why would Giana be handing out something like that here? What good will a bunch of teens do for the Cystic Fibrosis Foundation? I race back and forth between anger and nervousness. Angry that she'd do that, nervous that people will be able to figure out my secret.

I know people should be aware. I've been taught that my whole life. My mom and I participate in the Great Strides walks each year. We help with fundraising and we spread the

71

news, but not with people I see every day. There are a lot of CFers out there that are open about their disease, but it's something I've struggled with my whole life.

Another cough attack hits during first period. It rattles in my chest and surges out of my mouth. Over and over. I drink from my water bottle but it doesn't help for long. Which means I have to drink more and have to visit the bathroom all the time. Just what I need.

Before Kyler can even close his backpack at the end of class, I'm gone, out the door and down the hall to visit the bathroom before second period. I didn't even give him a chance to talk to me...maybe tell me something sweet that would calm my inner battle.

Right before I step into statistics, Max stops me outside the door. This time I'm really tempted to use the fist I spared on Jack.

"Did you hear?" Max asks.

I glance in the room and see Kyler already at his desk. My legs itch to move on, but Max places a hand across the doorway. I give a quiet, frustrated sigh. "Hear what?"

"That—"

"If you're going to say anything about Jack, I just might hurt you."

His hands fly up in surrender and he presses his lips together for a quick moment. "Nope. Didn't say a word. Don't know what you're talking about."

"Fine."

His hands drop. "There's a new kid."

The response in my head is somewhere along the lines of thanking him for informing me so I can eat lunch on the other side of the...planet. Seriously? "What's it with so many

72

new kids here? I thought I was weird transferring schools mid-year."

"New apartments in the school boundaries."

With all the anger built up inside me, a little bully bashing might just be what I need. "Okay, spill."

"Sophomore boy. Dark skin, kind of tall, goes by Mo."

I lift a brow and wonder if he's in much danger at all. Maybe he's good looking and Vivian will just stick to flirting and not bullying. "Okay. I'll see what I can do."

He shifts to the side. "Can't I help?"

I pat his shoulder and step past him, into the room. "I'll let you know."

Kyler must've heard my voice because his eyes are on us when I finally break away. The teacher is making his way around the room, placing a full sheet of paper on each desk. Before I sit down, he says, "Pop quiz. Take a seat and we'll start right when the bell rings."

I sink into my chair and glance at Kyler. He smiles and I let my eyes linger on his lips until I find his freckle. There it is. Small, brown, inviting. Wait. Did I just think that? I look up to see Kyler's gaze on me, watching me stare at his lips. Heat inches across my cheeks and down my neck. My insides squirm and a rush of flutters bloom in my chest.

The bell rings, announcing the time to stop the frantic thoughts and start the quiz. For some reason, I can't focus. Well, it's a perfectly good reason, but the teacher probably wouldn't be happy about it. In fact, by the end of class, I decide he's not happy about anything. The lesson today is long and boring and goes over the bell.

I'm packing my bag when someone touches my arm.

73

"Hey Kate," Kyler says. He steps toward the door and I freeze. "See you at lunch."

A slight nod of my head and he's gone. He's racing out of the room, his footsteps matching each thump pounding my chest.

* * *

Right when lunch starts, I head towards Giana's locker. Halfway there, I stop at the drinking fountain to kill a coughing fit. Either the air is super dry today or…no, I won't think about the other reason I would be coughing. It's got to be the air.

Giana is just shutting her locker when I arrive. I catch my breath and grab the flyer in her hand. "What's this all about?" I still haven't decided whether to be mad or happy about it.

She's beaming. "Isn't it great? I learned online that the best way to help is to spread the word."

"At school?"

There's hope in her eyes. "Everywhere. And since I'm always here, I figured it'd be a good place to start."

I return the flyer and run my fingers through my hair with a sigh.

"Relax, Kate. No one's going to know you have it just from this."

I scan the hallway to make sure no one hears us. "I know. Anyway, we've got something else to worry about."

"Really?"

I shrug. "Worry if you want. Max *informed* me of a new student."

She taps her chin. "I guess we'd better get to the cafeteria then."

74

This is another thing I haven't decided yet. Do I help or stay away? Giana takes off down the hall and I decide to follow. Which, I guess, means that I've decide to help.

One step into the cafeteria and I *know* we've missed Vivian's first move. She has Mo backed into a corner. Her flirt charm is on high: her blue-streaked hair pulled in a side bun, fresh lip gloss applied, leaning forward in her low V-neck shirt. I glance at Giana to find her head tilted, eyes on Mo. Like *really* on him, can't look away, might have a sudden crush on his chocolate-colored skin, deep eyes...

Giana sighs. Mo's arms are folded and he glances past Vivian. He seems bored. His gaze lands on us and Giana snaps out of it.

"Come on." I pull her forward and she stumbles behind me. A few more steps and a painful cough pushes up my throat. I stop in place and cover my mouth with the crook of my elbow. Now Giana's attention is on me. She holds my shoulder with one hand and pats my back. When I straighten up, concern fills her eyes.

"You okay?" she asks.

I swallow and cringe at the pinch of pain in the back of my throat. I must've coughed too hard. "I think so."

"We could go—"

"Giana. It's fine." I already have a mom worrying about me and I worry enough for everyone else. "Let's go."

By the time we make it closer to Vivian, Mo's starting a conversation with her. "What's your name?" he asks.

She flutters her lashes and folds her arms under her chest. "Viv."

Giana and I turn to each other and mouth the shortened version of her name with raised eyebrows. Oh, this boy is definitely getting new-kid torture—just a different kind than any of us got. I'm pretty sure Vivian didn't go that far trying to get Max on her side. Thank goodness, because I didn't need a constant replay of those details.

"What should we do?" Giana asks.

I bite my lip and try to decide if I should do something or do nothing. This is actually entertaining. But I can tell by the worry creasing Giana's forehead that she doesn't approve.

"I'll distract *Viv*," I say, batting my lashes. "You go save the poor boy."

Giana's eyes light up and her cheeks flush pink. I turn and we split ways. I approach Vivian from the side and get a slight grin from Mo. Vivian glances over her shoulder and freezes. I walk up casually and lean on a nearby table. "Hey, *Viv*."

Her face turns rigid. "What do you want?"

I shrug a shoulder. "Not much. Just thought I'd stop and say hi." My next breath gets caught in the painful spot in my throat and tries to come back out. I swallow hard to keep it down.

Vivian drums her fingers on her folded arms and stares at me. She forces a smile and says, "Hi."

I turn to Mo. "You must be the new kid."

He chuckles. "Word travels fast."

He has *no* idea. Max enters the cafeteria. Shoot. Gotta finish this before he tries to "help." Giana's moved closer, but she's hesitant. Apparently it's harder for her to do much of anything around Mo. I stand straight. "Hey, Mo. See that girl over there?"

His gaze follows my pointed finger to Giana. He nods.

"She's part of the unofficial meet and greet committee for new kids. Have you met her?"

"Nope."

I laugh, a fake, airy giggle. Giana eyes me and I let the laugh linger. "Looks like she's waiting for you. It was nice to meet you, though."

Vivian's glare cuts daggers straight for me. The second Mo steps away, she gets right up in my face. Or, really, I should say down in my face since she's basically bending over. "What was that all about?"

"Oh, puh-lease." I roll my eyes. "How would Jack feel if he knew you were flirting with another boy?"

"Jack's dead to me."

"That's a shame."

She grunts. "What are you talking about?"

I step to the side to get out of her space, or to get her out of mine. "Because Jack and I didn't really make out." I turn around and walk away.

Not a minute later, Kyler comes in and waves me over to an empty table. I sit beside him.

"This has been a crazy day," he says.

"Agreed." My answer is instant, but true.

"Look, I've been wanting to—"

I sneeze and scramble for a tissue. I'm wiping my nose and coughing and dreading the truth. Either Jack gave me his cold or someone else did. I can't even enjoy this moment with Kyler. A few more wretched coughs scratch their way up my throat and I take a long drink from my water bottle.

"Sorry." My response comes out hoarse.

Kyler touches my arm. "Are you okay?"

I take a deep breath and wipe my nose again. "I think so."

He pauses for a second. His cheeks turn a shade of red. "Do you want to go on a date with me?"

I blink a few times and try to process his words. Once I do, I swallow, try to breathe, finally manage a few quick breaths and end up coughing again. When the worst passes, I shake my head.

"You don't?" The pain in his eyes cuts to my heart. It's like I've taken his favorite song and changed the notes to an off-key, distorted melody.

"No. I mean yes." What do I mean? Yes, I'd love to? I clench my teeth and think about what's holding me back. A few more coughs give me time to come up with the right answer. "I'm not saying no. What I'm trying to say is…" Heat creeps across my cheeks and my thoughts scatter. *Ugh.* Why can't I think straight? My nose drips and I get another tissue. "I think I'm sick."

A sliver of relief softens his piercing eyes. "Maybe another time?" He tilts his head and offers a small smile.

I can't do anything but nod. I'm afraid if I talk, it's going to have repercussions. My keys jingle as I get them out of my backpack.

"Where are you going?"

"Home," I whisper.

If I'm really sick, Mom's going to flip. I might actually see those black belt skills if this cold doesn't kill me first.

Chapter 11

It's hard not to focus on the fact that I turned down a date with Kyler. Singing Kyler, the one whose voice melts my worries, takes me to faraway places, and makes me feel more alive than any breathing treatment. It's exactly what I need right now, but no one wants to be near me when I'm coughing this hard.

My chest aches, my throat's on fire, and the pounding in my head won't go away. I call Mom the second I get home from school and tell her the bad news. Or rather, cough her ear off until she understands and hangs up. I drink water and go to my room for some treatments. Something's better than nothing. I strap the percussion vest around my body and decide to use the nebulizer at the same time. Usually, all of this helps suppress a persistent cough.

But this time it doesn't.

I call Mom again.

"Mom." Cough.

"Kate, have you done your percussion therapy?"

I struggle to respond. "Yes."

"Nebulizer?"

Another cough. "Yes."

79

"Put your shoes on and wait by the front door. I'll call the doc on my way home and we'll go straight to his office."

I knew she'd say something like that. You'd think I'd be used to seeing Doctor Perry by now, but I'm not. My skin tingles and my muscles twitch. What is he going to say? Infection? Collapsed lung? It's suddenly hard to breathe…which makes the ache in my head spin. I can do this. It's just an infection. It has to be. This isn't one of those times I want to prepare for the worst.

Mom's home in no time. She honks and I hurry to the car, water bottle in one hand and travel tissue pack in the other. The faint leather scent inside her car tickles my nose and I sneeze.

"Tell me your symptoms," Mom says.

I run through the list and she nods. Mom studies cystic fibrosis and the recurring sicknesses that go with it more than I ever will. It would just give me more to think about, and dread. This time, she doesn't tell me her prediction. Her eyes are on the road, mouth pressed tight, and arms stretched out straight. I breathe in and out. In and out.

I close my eyes and find Kyler there. I focus on his face and try to tune out the rasp that rattles my chest with each breath. His voice fills my head, it seeps through my body and calms my racing heart. I imagine him taking my hand, sliding his fingers through mine, pulling me gently down a cobbled street. A violin plays softly in the distance and a muted *clink clink* of wine glasses accompanies the soothing sound of French people chattering. My head sinks back and I can finally breathe a little better.

"We're here." Mom's voice kills the image and my heart rate speeds back up.

A bead of sweat trickles down my back. I open the car door and rush to keep up with Mom's quick steps. She's not much taller than me, but when she's on a mission, her strides can outpace anyone with long legs. We walk into the doc's office and a blast of cool air chills the moisture on my back. A shiver runs through me as I take in the smell of meds, old people, cleaner, and some kind of tropical air freshener. The combination makes my stomach churn and I sit down with another round of coughs.

The stiff fabric beneath me doesn't give. It doesn't comfort or help me relax one bit. Mom checks me in and the nurse shows up a minute later.

As we follow her back, I walk with stiff legs so my feet don't tremble. We pause at a scale and the nurse gestures for me to step on the low, black box. Even with all my clothes, I weigh less than the last time I was at the doc's. I cough into my handful of tissues and grab the water bottle from my mom to take a drink. We proceed down the hall and turn into a room: small counter with a sink, containers filled with med supplies, upper cupboard next to a rectangular window. I've never been to prison, but it's like I've just walked into a cell. Again. My mom settles in the only chair and the nurse turns to me.

"Why don't you have a seat on the bed and I'll take your blood pressure."

I place my foot on the pull-out step and hoist my body onto the bed. The paper cover crinkles beneath me and I hold still. The way my heart's racing, they're sure to admit me into the hospital for something. The nurse fastens the blood pressure cuff around my bicep and places her stethoscope on the crook of my arm. Air pushes the fabric against my skin

81

until I think my arm might pop. Then it releases a little at a time. My pulse beats a steady rhythm. *Pump pump pump* against the cool metal circle.

When it's finished, the nurse pulls back with a flat expression. Everything is going so slow. Why can't she move faster? I can't breathe right. She grabs a PFT reader from the counter and sticks it in my mouth to test my lung function levels. Once I've breathed on the device three times, she takes it out and records the results.

My body wracks with another cough and it seems like ten more minutes before Doctor Perry finally shows up.

He presses his pointer fingers together and says, "Tell me how you feel."

I repeat my symptoms and he nods once before checking my file.

"I'm guessing it's just an infection," he says. "But with your recent history, that can be dangerous in itself."

I swallow hard and glance at Mom. Her eyes are locked on the doc and her knee bounces up and down quickly.

Doc Perry adjusts his glasses. "I'm going to prescribe an antibiotic similar to the one that treated your last infection." He turns back a few pages. Yes, my file is *that* long. Almost like its own book of diseases—a record of all the things that are slowly killing my body. "Looks like it's worked a few times before."

Mom sighs. "How do you want her to take it?"

"I'm going to prescribe an inhaler." The doc turns back to us and folds his arms over his rounded belly. "Before you pick it up, I want you to stop by the hospital for a chest x-ray."

I flinch. "But I thought you said it was just an infection." An uneasy feeling seeps through me. I don't want to go to the hospital, even if it's just a short visit.

"We can't tell for sure until some tests are done. Infection would be best case scenario at this point. We have to make sure your lungs are at full capacity and check to see if there is a collapse in one of the bronchioles. We also need to draw some blood for a few tests."

I cringe and close my eyes. Needles, x-rays, tests—it reminds me too much of my last stay in the hospital. I thought I wouldn't be afraid anymore, but the truth is, I'm petrified. I just act tough so I can push it away and live a somewhat normal life. As much as I hated going to that party with Giana, I'd much rather face that group of kids than go to the hospital. Even if I had to kiss every single one of those boys. At least I'd know I'd come out alive. Every time I go to the hospital, I'm afraid it will be the last time.

"Thank you, Dr. Perry," Mom says. She's all business. This is what happens whenever we get a diagnosis. If she cuts herself off emotionally, she won't have to think about the details. It's all about focus. Focus on fixing the problem, getting the right medicine, making sure I don't die.

Mom leads me to the car and we hurry to the hospital. It takes all my will-power to walk inside. The minute I do, I completely shut down. I guess, like Mom, it's my way of surviving the flat x-ray table, the prick of a needle, the waiting line for the inhaler, the exhaustion...life. This is how I survive. Fight or flight. I'm constantly fighting, but sometimes my brain takes flight so it can't focus on what's happening.

Even though this is just another infection, and even though the x-ray and blood tests come back normal, it's only

83

normal for now. Every infection breaks me down, pulls me apart, makes me realize why I didn't want to connect with Giana and Kyler. And makes me even more upset that I already have.

I'm okay with dying...I *thought* I was okay with dying. I'm glad that for now, I just have an infection. I get to live another day, another moment listening to Kyler, dreaming about what could be.

My finger pushes down on the inhaler and I breathe in the meds. The doc says to call back if I'm not doing better within a few days. And he says to go to the hospital if I get any worse. I won't feel worse. I can't.

Chapter 12

I've been stuck in the house for twenty-four hours and have to get outside before mom comes home from work. I stumble out of bed, throw on a coat and hat, and grab my inhaler. A chilly breeze greets me as I walk out the front door and head to a nearby park. The sun's warmth battles the winter air and seeps into my skin. I breathe in, willing the fresh air to clean my lungs—to kill this infection and give me a chance to finish high school.

A chance to go on a real date with Kyler, not just another fake one in my head.

It's only a few blocks to the park, but a cough attack hits me halfway there and I consider going back. Sure, I've got my French pictures in my room, not to mention a handful of documentaries I haven't seen in a while, but I need *this*. To be outside in the fresh air.

A dog barks close by and I turn the corner. Once the park is in sight, a black lab runs away from me, back to its owner. Past them sits the playground with a few green slides, a swaying bridge, and three swings. I zip my coat higher and head toward the swings. Their simple, gentle movement usually relaxes me and tends to encourage my imagination.

I snuggle onto the cool seat and close my eyes. I inhale deeply, letting the air pierce my lungs. It stings my throat on the way out, but I do it again. In and out, back and forth. My fingers tighten around the inhaler, keeping it safe as I lift higher into the air. I lean back and push forward, the air rushes across my face.

The Sainte Chapelle fills my head, the colorful stained glass swirling with elaborate patterns, the spires piercing the sky above. I'm walking through it, staring at the arches, listening to Kyler's voice whisper in my ear. Instead of turning toward him, I face forward and continue my even breaths. In, out, back and forth. If I look at him, he might not actually be there. Or maybe the way I imagine his face won't be close enough to the real thing. His voice, I could never get wrong. So I listen, and breathe, and somewhere inside, I know I'm really on a swing, slowing down, grasping onto the one thing that will save me if I start coughing too hard.

"Kate?"

That's funny. Of all the times I've imagined Kyler, he's never said my name. Especially with so much clarity. But I don't want to lose that, so I close my eyes tighter.

"Kate."

His voice sounds so real.

"Are you okay?"

My eyes fly open and I almost fall out of the swing. Kyler's standing in front of me, almost as if my dreams had become reality.

"How long have you been there?" I ask.

"Not that long."

"Oh." My mind's frantic, trying to snap back to real life. "Aren't you supposed to be at school?"

86

Kyler sits on a swing and turns toward me. "Free period. How about you?"

"Sick."

"Shouldn't you be inside?"

I shrug. "Inside can get boring real fast. But you're right. I should probably head back soon." I cough a few times in my arm and an ache flares in my chest.

"You need a ride?" Kyler asks.

"No." I clear my throat. "I don't live very far." I glance toward my house then look back at Kyler. He has a playful smile and his curly hair is ruffled by the wind...just like my insides are ruffled by him being here. "What are you doing at the park anyway?"

He focuses on his feet as they push through the bark chips. "I come here every once in a while."

I face him, our toes a few inches apart. "Why?"

He shrugs and closes his mouth. The silence leaves me hanging, wanting to know more about this boy who has worry lines across his forehead.

The lines deepen and I clench my teeth to keep quiet. Kyler finally looks up and stares past me, toward the play set. His voice is quiet when he says, "My mom used to bring me here when I was a little boy."

And he keeps coming back so he can remember her. My chest tightens and the ache seems to grow. Kyler came here to think of his mom and instead he's talking to me. It's almost like I'm intruding on their personal time. I turn away and lean forward to stand up.

"Where are you going?"

"I just...I thought maybe you'd like to be alone."

Kyler moves his leg closer and taps my foot with his. "Don't go."

The energy racing up my leg soars through my heart and steals my words. I blink twice and manage to say, "You sure?"

"Yes. I'm sick of being alone. Sometimes it's nice to have people around me."

I chuckle.

The pain in Kyler's face eases and his eyes light up. "Did I say something funny?"

"You always have people around you." Unlike me, but that's my choice.

"They're just people. Ever since my mom passed away, it's been hard to connect with them. Most of them don't know what it's like to lose someone. They go through life taking so much for granted. It's really frustrating sometimes."

I nod, stuck somewhere between losing someone and taking everything for granted. I've always pushed people away because of myself. Kyler's *really* trying to fit in, but it isn't working. So why does he want to be friends with me? Can he tell I'm different? Maybe he knows I have a secret since I isolate myself and scare people away instead of trying to fit in. Maybe he likes a good challenge—that's why he wants to be friends so bad. Not that I'm complaining.

"Hey," Kyler says, making me focus. "Let's do something fun."

I cough in response. Yeah, it's totally hot. "Like what? I can't stay out much longer."

He stands up and comes behind me. "Let's live in this moment. Like we're still little kids."

He grabs my swing and I cling to the chains to keep steady. He pushes me forward and I feel like I'm living a dream. I laugh, and cough, and listen to Kyler's voice as he sings a nursery rhyme about money, and getting ready, and go. He pushes me hard and I'm flying. And coughing again. I need to stop, to get a good breath, but Kyler keeps pushing. I wrap my arms around the chains and try to hold still long enough to use my inhaler. Between the swing moving and the cough shaking my body, I can't get it to work.

"Stop," I scream, my voice hoarse.

Kyler stops me so hard, I almost land on my face. I lean back and shove the inhaler in my mouth. I push the button on top and suck the medicine in. Kyler's apologizing and rubbing my back. Once the medicine is in me, I can finally breathe.

"I'm really sorry," he says again.

"It's not your fault. I should really get home, though. I'll be lucky if my mom lets me go to school tomorrow."

Kyler reaches down and gives me a hand. "Is it that bad?"

Bad? How can anything be bad when his hand is in mine? I shake my head and think of France, happy times, being a kid…anything but the fact that I'm already standing and he still has my fingers in his grip.

A small cough escapes and reminds me that I have a reason to push everyone away. I'd hate to make a connection. I let go and hold my inhaler between both hands.

"You sure you don't want a ride?" he offers again.

"Yeah…thanks though."

"Can I walk you home?"

89

I should say no, but what's another five minutes together? I try not to look too happy as I say, "I guess."

Maybe I'll get another offer for that date I turned down.

Or maybe not. Kyler does most of the talking—telling me about his childhood. The only time he mentions his mom is when he talks about the way his dad acted after she died. "He wanted to move," Kyler says. "He needed a fresh start and didn't want to be reminded of her every time he turned a corner."

"Why didn't you leave?"

"I told him I didn't want to go." He lifts his hands with the short explanation and lets them fall. "I *couldn't* go."

We're in front of my house now so I stop. "But it's so hard for you to be around your friends and everything. Do you think it would've been better in the long run?"

Kyler's gaze roams my face and he presses his lips together. I hold my breath and hope this moment doesn't get ruined by another cough attack.

"No." He shakes his head, but his eyes never leave mine. "Definitely not."

"Why?" I whisper.

"Because if I had left, I wouldn't be able to visit the park. I need those memories. I don't want to lose her—don't want to forget. You know?"

I nod, even though I'm not quite sure I really know. I don't have memories of my dad. Nothing reminds me of him except for my fear of relationships, and that's something I'd like to forget.

"Besides," Kyler says. "If I'd moved, we wouldn't have played at the park together."

I laugh and his soft chuckle makes everything seem like it won't be so bad. "Thanks, Kyler. I'm feeling better already."

"Then maybe I'll see you tomorrow?"

The hope in his voice is so intense; it wraps around my nerves and squeezes them until I give the right answer. "Sure."

His face relaxes. "Good. Now go rest. If you're not there tomorrow, I might stop by since I know where you live now."

I stare at him, trying to decide if he's serious. Giana coming to my house is one thing, but Kyler? I'm not sure I can handle that yet.

"Bye," I say. I walk backward and watch Kyler as he stands there, keeping an eye on me until I close my front door. As much as I want to peek through the window, I don't. Instead, I lean against the door and hold onto the hope coursing through me. If Kyler wants me to be at school tomorrow, I'll make my sickness go away so I can be there.

Chapter 13

Mom's hesitant to let me go back Friday morning, but I really am feeling a little better. I'm not completely healed, but at least I'm not any worse. When I walk into psychology five minutes late, Kyler turns around and grins. I've got an inhaler in my backpack and an extra pack of tissues that Mom insisted I take—just in case.

Once class is over, Kyler's at my desk, gripping the strap on his bag and offering a smile that would make the gargoyles on Notre Dame happy. "Are you okay?"

I cough a little in response. "I think so."

I wonder what the story was. New girl gets Jack's cold and is out for three days.

Kyler steps back to let me out of my seat. "Bad cold, huh?"

I laugh, a hoarse, mucous-filled sound. It's disgusting. But Kyler keeps smiling as he leads the way to statistics. "Seriously," I say, "If I ever kiss another guy, he has to sign a waiver first. No more sharing sicknesses."

Kyler chuckles and it brightens my mood. I think of berets and sun dresses and walks through a manicured garden. "I'd like to see that," he says and I almost think he means my daydream. But really it's the consent form. "Can you imagine?"

I picture a boy with curly hair and freckles coming in for a kiss. In my hand is a piece of paper and a pen. It totally ruins the moment, but I enjoy the possibility. "Okay, maybe no signature. But maybe no more kissing either."

Kyler pauses and it takes me a second to turn around. His tooth digs into his lip so hard, I think it's about to bleed.

"Kyler."

He shakes his head. "Sorry."

Sorry about what? He stopped just after I said no more kisses. Does he want to kiss me? A cough races up my throat and I lean away until it subsides.

"Look," he says, his hands now relaxed by his sides. "I know you're still sick, but there's something I want to take you to tonight."

"A date?" I ask. That fake kiss springs to life in my head.

"You could call it that. Or we could just go as friends."

I tilt my head to the side. If I'm going anywhere with him, it's definitely a date. I'm just not sure my mom will be open to me hanging out in public with the chance of getting another infection. "Can you tell me where we're going?"

Kyler scratches his head. "I want it to be a surprise. I'm not sure you'll even like it, but I think you will."

"Will there be a lot of people?" He shakes his head and I grin—which probably makes it look like I *want* to be alone with him. "I'll go. What time?"

"I'll be by around six thirty." We step into the statistics room and Kyler stops me before I make it to my seat. "Is this a date or are we just going as friends?"

93

A pounding in my chest steals my thoughts. I fight back for them and sort through the chaos. I was hoping he wouldn't ask about this detail. Basically my answer will tell him how I really feel. And I'm not sure I want him to know that yet. I'm not sure I'm even ready to admit it to myself. The pounding surges toward my throat and I swallow. The words come out in a whisper. "Can it be both?"

One side of Kyler's mouth lifts into a smoldering half-smile. He reaches forward and barely brushes my hand with his fingertips. Tingles spread up my arm and cut off my air. I'm not breathing, not thinking, not moving. Just floating toward my seat in a dreamy trance. Like he's put me under some kind of spell that mashes my insides together and leaves me completely helpless.

I don't know what the lesson's about in class today. And I think Max waves at me on my way out the door, but I'm too focused on Kyler to wave back.

Now that Kyler's walking down the hall beside me, I try to snap out of the haze. A cough forces its way to my mouth and makes my eyes burn. There's yucky stuff coming up my throat. I give him a lame excuse to find water and instead hurry to the bathroom. The coughing doesn't stop until I use my inhaler. Even then, the tickle at the back of my throat persists on bothering my lungs. A sharp pain pinches my throat every time I swallow. The meds will work. I just need to drink more water and maybe avoid talking so much.

* * *

At lunch, I find Giana eating next to Mo. I make my way through the lunch line and glance around the room for Kyler. Instead of finding him, I catch Vivian staring at Mo. The usual

94

boys surround her at the table but she's ignoring them, her lips pursed as she taps her chin with a long finger.

"Vivian's got the hots for you, Mo." I sit next to Giana and glance at Vivian. Her stony face turns down and her minions scramble for her attention. The moment distracts Mo long enough for me to slip my pills in my mouth and drink them down.

"Looks like she's got enough attention," Mo says with a chuckle. "She shouldn't miss me much."

Giana turns to me. "Mo and I were just talking about this weekend. You have any plans?"

I take a bite of food and nod. Giana stares, clearly waiting for me to go on. I shrug and can't help the smile tugging at my lips.

"Come on," she says. "Hot date?"

The room grows warm and I almost choke on my food with a rising cough. Even when it settles, she's still waiting. And now Mo is too.

"Yes," I say, lifting my hands in surrender. "Hot date tonight. In fact I have three more tomorrow. Busy weekend, you know. But that's normal."

Giana laughs and Mo lifts an eyebrow in confusion.

"Seriously, Kate." Giana takes a bite of her turkey wrap. "Do you want to hang out with us?"

I shrug. "I'm not sure what I have going on tomorrow. Mom was really reluctant to let me come to school with my cold." My gaze drills through the air toward Giana in a "you know...still worried about the lungs and all" kind of stare. "How about you guys plan something and let me know what it is. I should know by tomorrow morning if I'm free."

"Sounds good."

95

A few minutes later, Mo gets up to refill his water bottle and I lean toward Giana. "How's it going?"

She fakes a confused look. Totally fake. People don't look happy when they're that confused. "What do you mean?"

"Don't give me that, Giana. Mo seems to like you."

She lets out a short, defeated laugh. "Or he just doesn't know anyone else."

"Whatever. He totally does."

Giana raises a shoulder and lets it fall. "I hope so. Nothing major yet."

"And how's your niece?"

Her smile goes limp. "Good. I guess. I mean..." She rubs her forehead. "As good as she can be. She's a happy baby."

"And lucky to have an aunt who's going to find a cure." Giana's earlier enthusiasm has obviously died down. "How's your sister holding up?"

She sighs. "She's either in denial or accepting life. She loves her baby but I can see how worried she is."

I nod. That worry will never go away. Even with all the good times, it will still be there, hidden in the dark corners of her mind. But I don't say this to Giana. Mo's coming back so I give her something else to smile about. "By the way," I say. "I wasn't kidding about that date tonight. Kyler's taking me somewhere."

"Seriously?" Her face lights up and she's smiling like no one in the world could even have a crazy disease, especially not someone so close to her.

"Yeah, now..." I close my lips and tilt my head toward Mo, who's taking his seat.

Giana turns to him and I'm glad she's chipper again. She may not know it, but Mo seems to look at her as some kind of angel. The way he talks, the way his eyes roam over her face whenever she's not looking. Yeah, there's definitely something there. Even if it's only been a few days. Love at first sight, right? Giana was totally smitten the moment she saw him. Maybe it's a two way thing.

I finish my lunch and get up to leave. Giana puts a hand on my arm and says, "Have a *good day*." She even adds a wink to put more emphasis behind her words. Yes, yes. I hope to have a fun time on my date tonight.

* * *

Around six o'clock, my mom comes in my room and sits on the edge of my bed. I'm at the tail end of percussion therapy and still need to finish getting ready for my date.

"You sure he's not taking you somewhere with a lot of people who could be sharing a lot of germs?"

I shake my head and focus on the air pounding my chest. My cough wasn't much better this afternoon and I don't want to be hacking up a lung on Kyler's lap.

"You'll take your inhaler, right? And cell phone?"

"Mom, you're acting like I've never been on a date."

"Well…" She doesn't finish because we both know it's been a long time. I could count the total number of dates on one hand. I'm surprised she's not doing my hair or helping me get ready. This is what she wants, for me to hang out, feel those feelings, make lots of friends. "Is he a nice boy?" she asks.

"Remember the boy we saw at the grocery store last week?"

Her eyes light up.

"That's him. And, yes, he's nice. Why do you think I agreed to go with him at all?" I fix my eyes on her. "Please don't threaten him with your black belt like my last date."

Mom laughs. "That was over a year ago, honey."

I give her a pointed look. "Yes. I know. It scared all the other boys away." Not that there were very many…or any at all. I'm not sure why I'd agreed to go on the day anyway. He definitely wasn't my type.

Her laugh grows. "Well, they should know not to put the moves on you. I didn't even have to do anything. In fact, he probably still has bruises from the wounds you gave him."

I flinch. She's probably right. Maybe not physical bruises but emotional ones. It's not every day a guy gets beat up by his date. I pick up a dart and throw it at the target. It hits the mark and my therapy timer rings. I turn off the machine and unstrap the vest.

"I have to get ready, Mom. You can meet Kyler when he comes to get me."

Her eyes linger on me as she walks backwards out of the room. Yes, I know I'm eighteen. And this is what my mom wants. But I still think it's hard for her to let me go. To know that I may get attached to a boy and that my time with her will be shared with someone else.

* * *

Kyler shows up a few minutes early, which gives him bonus points in my mom's eyes. She's always reminding me that it's better to run early than be late.

He's wearing dark, fitted jeans with a plain t-shirt showing beneath his open jacket. His curls are gelled into perfect springs and the freckles near his eyes squeeze together when he smiles. He reaches a hand toward Mom. "I'm Kyler."

98

Mom takes his hand, all business-like, and shakes it hard. "You won't be out too late, right?"

"*Mom*," I whisper. Those are the same words she used right before telling my last date about her part-time karate job. Luckily, this time, Mom backs away with a wink.

"We'll be back by nine," Kyler says then he leads me out the door to a fancy car in our driveway.

I give a low whistle. "Is this yours?"

He chuckles. "My dad let me use it."

I run my hand along the metallic silver. "That's…nice of him."

Kyler opens my door and goes around to his side. The second he starts the car, a grin stretches across his face. "Dad only lets me borrow it for dates."

"Wait. This is a date?" I ask, half joking. But we did decide that it was a date as friends. At least, that's what I thought.

There's a playful look in Kyler's eyes as he takes off down the road. "My dad thinks it is."

"Let me guess. You haven't had a chance to drive it in a while and I looked like a nice girl to ride with."

Kyler takes one hand off the wheel and reaches across the console. His fingers trail along my arm until they reach my hand. Then he pauses. And I'm about to die from lack of breath. My pulse is pounding against my wrist and I'm almost positive that's why his hand stopped. He can probably feel the erratic rhythm beneath my skin.

"Is there a consent form for hand holding?" he asks.

A laugh forms in me and I can't hold it back. It fills my mouth and comes out as a violent cough. I lean away to divert the worst of it, but Kyler's fingers slide between mine.

99

He holds on and I squeeze back. The cough was more than just a slight tickle and I'm scrambling in my purse with my free hand to get a tissue. I grab the pack of travel Kleenex and also bring out a water bottle.

And now I have to let go of Kyler, just long enough to get things under control.

The second my hand leaves his, he asks, "You sure you're okay?"

I nod and take a long swig of water.

"I can take you back home if you're not feeling well enough yet."

"No," I say quickly. "It should be fine. The doc gave me medicine for this cold, but it's just taking a while to go away."

"Positive?"

I clean the germs with a squirt of disinfectant and reach for Kyler's hand. Hopefully that's a good enough answer for him. "Are you going to tell me where we're going yet?"

His grip tightens. "No. But I did ask Giana for some ideas."

My jaw falls. "You did? I thought she didn't know about the date."

Kyler shrugs. "She's good at keeping secrets."

Of course she is. And she acted so surprised…or maybe she was just excited. She knew all along. Another cough kills the conversation and I decide it must be all the talking. Usually when I'm sick, I stay at home with Mom. We watch movies, play games, or mind our own business. None of that takes much talking.

Besides, it gives me more time to think about Kyler's hand in mine. I mean, *he's holding my hand*! That's a huge deal. I've held a few other hands, but none of them belonged to boys as charming as Kyler. He hums a soft melody and my insides turn to jelly. A tingle spreads across my shoulders and races down my arms. I close my eyes and lay my head against the headrest, sinking into a blissful frenzy. My body is relaxed, but my insides are having a party. Elephants are stomping across my heart while butterflies flitter with excitement in my stomach.

Not only do I think of France, but I think of a French celebration at night with Kyler next to me. The Eiffel Tower is lit in the distance and fireworks explode through the air in sparks of color. A sweet, vanilla scent fills my nose and I imagine my teeth sinking into a bite of crème brûlée.

It's perfect. Even with the persistent cough that's bent on ruining the moment.

Kyler's hum dies down and the car stops. "We're here."

I hesitate to open my eyes. I don't know where "here" is and the place in my head is so dreamy, there couldn't be anything better.

Kyler squeezes my hand. "Kate. Open your eyes."

I open them in anticipation...only to see a plain brick building with a handful of cars in the parking lot. "Where are we?"

Kyler chuckles. "Come on. You'll see."

He releases my hand to get out of the car, but takes it again once he gets my door open. I grab my purse and sling it over a shoulder as we head toward the building. A sign rests on an easel by the door, but I can't read it until we get closer.

Once I can make out the letters, I read:

Local Art Show. Jean de Chelles, Pierre de Montreuil, Matthias of Arras, and other period works: Gothic French art and architecture of the 13th century. No touching, please.

"Really?" I can't say anything else. An overwhelming sense of appreciation takes over my body and pricks my eyes with moisture. I swallow back a wave of gratitude and sniff into a tissue. Of all the places a teenage boy would want to go on a date, I imagine this is the last one. How did he know about it anyway? I'd ask him, but I'm afraid to open my mouth. He tugs on my arm and we walk inside.

We enter a room separated with light gray partitions. Spotlights hang from the ceiling, shining on different works of art. I linger in front of the first painting and my daydream in the car comes to life. It's Paris at night with the Eiffel Tower lit up, reflected in the Seine River with watercolor squiggles. We move from one piece to another, some of them as big as the wall and others as small as my hand. There are sculptures of Notre Dame, palaces, and cathedrals.

Even though there are other people in the room, I feel like Kyler and I are alone.

"What do you think of this one?" he whispers in my ear and points to a wooden carving of the Gallery of Kings.

The twenty-eight kings are lined up, each one wearing a crown, holding a staff, and wearing a draped robe. The faces are turned down and the eyes are left blank—like the artist couldn't decide which emotion to portray. Or maybe they wanted the observer to see their own emotions. I turn to Kyler and find his eyes on me.

"It's beautiful, Kyler," I say quietly. His gaze travels down my face and pauses on my lips.

102

His mouth quirks up on both sides and he reaches a hand to my face. His finger leaves a burning trail along my skin as he tucks a strand of hair behind my ear. "You know, you don't say my name very often."

Maybe not to him, but it fills my mind all day. Even now, my heart is pounding his name through my body. My fingers ache to draw his name in patterns through his hair. And right at the tip of my tongue, his name is ready to be said. I lean closer and say it with a sigh. "Kyler."

It releases a million heart beats at once and leaves me weak, leaning closer and hoping he'll catch me in his arms. His hand wraps around my back and he pulls me forward until our stomachs touch. I breathe in deeply...too deep. Before I can push away, I cough into his shirt. I hoped it was a small cough, but it keeps going. One after another and I have to get away. I push against him and bend over. The cough curdles in my chest and rips its way out my throat.

"What can I do?" Kyler asks, panicked.

I struggle to respond. "Water."

He reaches inside my bag and pulls out my water bottle. Before he can get it open, a man approaches and says, "I'm sorry, but you'll have to take that outside."

I barely see Kyler's wild eyes before another cough takes over. "You've got to be kidding. She's practically choking."

The man folds his hands together and I close my fist into a tight ball. How can he be so calm? If I weren't on the verge of hacking up a lung, I'd show him my anger.

"I'm sorry," he says. "But we can't risk the art."

I curse the art and stumble toward the door with a fuming Kyler behind me. He leads me to the parking lot with a hand on my back. Before we make it outside, he shoves the water in my hand and tells me to start drinking. I guzzle the water but it doesn't suppress the urge to keep coughing.

"Kyler," I say, my chest aches and silver sparkles flash across my vision. "Inhaler."

Kyler digs through my purse and finally pulls it out. I stick the bottom end in my mouth and push on the top to release the meds. I breathe it in, and cough it out. Hopefully some of it is in my system rushing through my veins and attacking the infection. At least, that's what it's supposed to do. But maybe it's not working.

The coughing has subsided a little but I need to get home. "Kyler, I'm sorry about this."

He takes my hand and shakes his head.

Before he can respond, I say, "Please. I need to go home."

The request kills me because I don't want my time with Kyler to end. I don't want to go home, to face the reality of what might *really* be happening. But I need to. I need my mom to tell me what to do. She knows the answers. And if she doesn't, the doc knows. As much as I don't want to call Doc Perry, I hate to think about the consequences if I don't.

Chapter 14

Kyler drops me off at the door and Mom pulls me inside with her eyebrows drawn together in obvious worry.

"I'll take it from here, Kyler," she says with a pointed look. "Have a good night." She shuts the door in his face and I want to scream, but there's nothing left in me. I'm like an empty cave taken over by a raging storm. My body aches and there's an overwhelming pounding against the base of my skull.

Mom leads me to the couch and makes me lie down then touches her wrist to my forehead. "No fever. That's a relief."

I don't feel relieved.

"Your pulse is high, but that's to be expected after a coughing attack. Especially on a date."

Attack? More like an ongoing episode on a hot date. The hot part is important, along with the almost kiss. I close my eyes and let my heart pound with the memory. Another cough tries to escape my mouth, but it's weak. I curl over the pain in my chest and turn to my side.

"I'm calling Doc Perry," Mom says. "I'll be back in a minute."

I just lie there, keeping my body still. I try to forget the last ten minutes in order to focus on the few moments I had in Kyler's arms. Exhaustion is taking over my body and I fight against it to find the memory. There. In the protected part of my brain that holds my most precious moments. Mom taking me to a French boutique after a long hospital stay. The old lady that lived next to us supporting me at a CF walk. Giana giving me food on the first day of school. And Kyler taking my hand, searching my eyes like he can't wait to spend another second together. Like he can't wait to kiss me the way I was supposed to have my first kiss. However that's supposed to go.

But why does he care about me? What is there to like? He doesn't even know me. And what will happen when he finally does? I release the memory and fall into a daze. My chest convulses with a constant cough but I've grown distant, retreating into my safe zone. I tuck my thoughts into a bed of black blankets and think of nothing. No death, no life.

I'm not sure how long I sit there, but Mom finally returns.

"Can you sleep?" she asks.

I open my eyes and look up at her. A question forms in my head, something along the lines of trying to drive straight on a curvy road: not possible. But I don't ask because I don't have enough energy to get it out...or deal with her response. Instead I close my eyes again and shrug.

"Doc thinks you've overdone it."

My eyes open. That's it? Overdone it? I'd like to see him rest while someone's jumping on his chest.

"He wants you to get some sleep and see how you feel in the morning."

106

I already know how I'm going to feel. Rotten. I retreat back under those mental blankets and cough my way into a dreamless oblivion.

* * *

I'm awake the next morning before Mom comes in. In fact, I'm not sure how much time has passed. My head hurts too bad to open my eyes, but it could be mid-day. I'm still on the couch and even though my chest hurts and my throat's raw, I must've been able to sleep a little. The cough shakes me more awake and I know I need to get to my room for breathing treatments.

"You awake yet?"

I lift my eyelids and whisper, "I've been waiting for you to come in." The response tears at my throat.

"How are you?"

I wonder if I can do impromptu sign language. This one should be easy. I give her a big ol' thumbs down.

"Let's do your therapy and meds and see how you're doing after that."

Mom pulls me into a sitting position and gives me a handful of pills with a glass of water.

"By the way, Giana called this morning. I told her you're still sick and won't be able to do anything for a while."

Of course she called. She probably wanted the 411 on my *surprise* date with Kyler. And Mom basically gave it to her. Still sick. Can't do anything. That's how it ended.

Mom helps me off the couch and up the stairs to do my nebulizer meds. Then she straps on my vest and checks on me multiple times before it finishes. It's like she thinks something might happen in the middle of therapy. But whether that something is good or bad, I don't know. I stare at the poster on the wall and French artwork flashes through my mind from the art gallery. Pictures and sculptures of places that I love. Places I want to visit.

I swallow a dash of hope and realize last night might've been the closest I'll ever come to experiencing the real France. At least Kyler was there with me.

Mom opens the door and my timer goes off.

"Any better?"

I take off the vest and let it drop to the ground. My shoulders fall forward. "What do you think?"

She bites her lip, folds her arms, and stands with her head tilted. After a whole minute of staring at nothing, she finally snaps out of it. "I'm taking you back in. Your resistance tests haven't come back for this round of antibiotics, but I don't think they're working. I'm going to ask Doc to put you on something else."

I pull what's left of my sanity into a tight knot and hold onto it so it can't escape. Back to the doc's I go. Back to the prison cell and back to the hard bed with only a paper sheet to protect me from other people's sicknesses.

This time it's a different doctor, since Perry's out of the office. The new doctor's name doesn't stick in my memory. I stare at his white lab coat and breathe in. He places the PFT reader in my mouth to test my lung function and I exhale as long and hard as I can. Three times. The first test result is similar to the one I got at my last appointment, but the next two readings are lower.

"She's not getting any better," the doc says while studying my file.

"I think we need to change the antibiotics," Mom says.

It's like I'm living the same moment over and over. Like no matter how far I've come from one sickness, I still fall back to where I was. I hear the same results from the same tests and nothing ever really gets better. I know that's how it's going to be. But I hope every day that it will be different—that eventually, someone will find a cure and all my hope can turn into reality.

The doctor rubs his eyebrows. "She needs a stronger antibiotic and it's going to have to be through an IV."

Mom's face goes rigid. "Hospital or home treatment?"

The doctor's gaze flicks to Mom and then his eyes focus on my face. "She looks pretty tired. Is she getting enough rest at home?"

"She can." I know Mom doesn't want me stuck in the hospital. But if she can't convince the doctor that I'll get everything I need at home, it will be a lost battle.

"What about all the IV treatments and extra therapy? Can you help her with those?"

Extra therapy. How do they expect me to get any rest at all? It doesn't matter if I'm at home or in the hospital.

"My work is flexible." Mom's face is relaxed but her hands are balled into fists. "I can come home when I need to and work while she's resting."

The doctor walks back to the small counter and sets my thick file down with a soft *thud*.

Mom shakes her hands out and folds them together. "I don't go back to work until Monday. Kate will have all my attention until then and every second I can give her after."

He turns around and eyes her with a stern look. "That's fine. But if she's not improving by then, we're going to have to admit her. She needs to get better or she'll be in the hospital for something far worse."

The weight of his statement settles over us in a heavy silence. Mom seems a little less tense and I'm thankful that she fought to keep me home. I can't go back to the hospital. Not yet. Even without treatments, I still wouldn't rest. How can I? Everything in the hospital reminds me of sickness. All I see is buttons and windows and nurses. I hear murmuring in the hall and think that everyone is talking about me. I worry that things aren't going right. At any moment they can come in and tell me I only have a few days left to live.

At home, I can pretend everything's okay. I have my architecture magazines, my light purple walls, and my darts. It distracts me and helps me calm down—only then can I get rest.

"You'll have to stop by the hospital for an initial treatment," the doctor says. "They'll send you home with all the IV medication."

Focus.

Breathe.

It's an initial treatment. It's not that bad. Go in, prick my arm, give me a dose of medicine, then walk out with everything else. I can do that. Mom stands up and shakes the doctor's hand. I slide off the bed and count the footsteps to the car.

Step. One... Step. Two...

All the way to forty-eight.

I focus on that number until I'm home. Forty-eight steps, forty-eight minutes in the hospital, forty-eight deep breaths in the car. Forty eight minutes past two in the afternoon.

I'm home. I'm alive. I'm going to be okay.

Chapter 15

By Monday morning, I'm still low on energy. The cough has subsided for the most part and the scratchy ache in my throat has gone away. I stay in bed and wait for Mom to come home for my next treatment. She set up the TV in my room and gave me a stack of documentaries on French architecture and classical artwork.

Someone knocks on my door. Not Mom. "Hello?"

"Kate. It's me, Giana. Can I come in?"

Giana? I pull up the blankets and fall into my pillow. "Sure."

The door inches open and she steps in. "Your mom called and said she wasn't going to make it home. She asked me to come by and check on you."

Really? Mom knows I can do my own IVs if I have to. Maybe she didn't want my friends to forget about me. I glance at the clock and see that it's lunchtime. "You really don't have to help."

"Your mom said you'd say that too." Giana folds her hands in front of her. "Actually, I asked how you were doing and she said I could stop by and see for myself."

I hold out my left arm and point to the PICC line needle imbedded in my skin. "As long as I keep up with my meds every six hours and do the added therapy, I'm fine. A little tired, but that's normal."

Giana nods. "Your mom said you needed a lot of rest."

"Yeah. It's definitely easier to heal when I'm not running around going on dates..." I lift my brow and press my lips together.

Giana throws her hands up. "Okay, okay. So I knew about the date." She pauses and crosses the room to sit on my chair. "Sorry it didn't end well. I didn't realize you were so sick."

I shrug and my mind flits back to the art gallery, to Kyler's intense gaze, to the way he reached so easily for my hand. I curl my fingers into a fist and squeeze the memory from my head. "I should've known better."

Giana twirls a strand of hair around her finger and offers a one sided, cheesy grin. "Did you have a good time with Kyler?"

Her smile spreads to the other side and I can't hold mine back any longer. "Stop that," I say, trying to suppress more giddiness from escaping. I laugh then cough. "Nothing happened."

I can call holding hands nothing, right? I mean, it *was* nothing. It's not like we kissed or anything. A sudden pounding takes over my chest and reminds me that it was anything *but* nothing. Heat crawls across my face and my breaths become shallow.

Giana's eyes are wide. "Nothing? That's not what it sounds like to me."

The thumping in my chest beats a constant rhythm on the growing knot in my stomach. What did she hear?

"Kyler keeps asking if I know how you're doing," she says. "He's really worried about you. And he wouldn't be that worried over nothing."

I exhale the air trapped in my lungs. Okay. So it wasn't like she heard anything specific. She's just making assumptions.

"Did anything happen?" Giana asks.

She didn't define "anything" so I shake my head. "By the way, thanks for telling him about my love for French architecture. How did you know?"

Giana points to the posters on my wall: Notre Dame, the Eiffel Tower, the Sainte Chapelle. "Just took a guess. And you're welcome."

A timer rings on my phone. I turn off the alarm and sit up. "Would you mind bringing me my meds?"

"Where are they?"

"Under the target in a container."

Giana gets out a bag of meds and brings it over. I hook it up and shiver as the cool liquid enters my body, slowly seeping through my veins. This is what I get to do all day, every day until this sickness goes away. Whether I'm at school or at home, this needle in my arm is a part of my life for now.

After a while, Giana leaves, to get to her next class. But tomorrow I'll be joining the throng of students. Mom says I've improved enough to return to school as long as I don't do anything crazy.

I fill my day with resting, reading, watching documentaries, doing extra therapy, and taking my meds. Hopefully there won't be any new kids at school tomorrow. I kind of think bully-fighting against Vivian would fall under crazy and there's only so much I'm willing to risk my life for.

* * *

Mom takes me to school the next morning and hands my meds to Nurse Molly. It's nice to know there's a place closed off from the rest of the school where I can be me. Nurse Molly knows all about my disease and also knows that I want to keep it as private as possible.

Mom brings her up to speed with my infection and then we all part ways. Mom goes to work but I'll be back with Nurse Molly after lunch. At home my drip line takes two hours, but I turn it on faster at school so I can finish in thirty minutes.

I turn down the hall toward my locker and find Kyler leaning against it. The smile on his lips makes my whole body feel light, alive.

"Giana told me you'd be here today." He reaches out and tugs lightly on the hem of my long-sleeved shirt.

Long sleeves to cover the PICC line opening for my IV meds—it's all carefully planned. I clear my throat and breathe in. "I'm here."

He steps closer and his finger trails down the side of my hand. I want to lean into him, but I just stand still. Kyler tilts his head down and his gaze pierces me, searching for something. I feel open and vulnerable, like he can see every secret I have. The one about my disease, the one about the needle in my arm, and the one that isn't much of a secret anymore—the way I feel about him. I'm sure that one's written on every part of my face.

"Are you okay?" he whispers.

His words steal my thoughts. I swallow hard and stare at his lips. They're parted, showing the tip of his tongue. I focus on his single freckle and my body sways forward. His lips close and I wonder if he wants to kiss me.

Wait. I'm in the *school hallway*. What am I thinking? This is the worst place to have a first kiss with someone. No doubt other kids have done it, but not me. I lean back and rack my brain to remember his question. I blink and find my answer. "I think so."

"Oh good." Kyler steps back and rubs his forehead. Is he sweating? Did he want that kiss as much as I did?

"Hey, Kate," someone says from behind me.

I close my eyes and picture my fist landing in *someone's* blue hair. What does Vivian want? My eyes open just in time to see her step into my line of vision and basically kill my conversation with Kyler.

"Heard you had a cold."

I shrug. Why would she care anyway?

"Maybe you learned your lesson."

Kyler leans back and stifles a laugh. I glare at him and fold my arms together. Yes, it's the only thing that keeps me from getting crazy. "What are you talking about, Vivian?"

She steps close and bends forward to get right in my face, popping any kind of personal bubble I might've had. "I don't want to see your lips on my man ever again."

I roll my eyes. "I thought we went over this."

"I'm just making sure we're clear in case you get any ideas."

I nod. Right. Clear. "Well, since we're pointing out the obvious, I'll show you how much I don't want your man." I lift my fist between us and Vivian's eyes bulge. She jumps

116

back as I stretch my fingers out. Her eyebrow shoots up and she cocks her head to the side. I grin, reach my hand toward Kyler's and grab hold of his fingers.

"Come on," I tell him. "Let's get to class."

Vivian's jaw drops and Kyler's laugh leads us down the hall.

"Why didn't you stand up for me?" I ask him, faking a frown and swinging our hands. "I thought she was going to bite off my face."

Kyler nudges my side. "I would've stopped her, but I know you'd win that fight any day."

That fight. The only one in my life I might be able to win. Too bad the other constant battle is one I can never overcome. The thought weighs on me and dampens the happiness from going public with Kyler—as public as walking halfway down the hall can be. Once we get to psychology, he breaks away and goes to his seat.

* * *

Somehow I missed Max in statistics. Even after Kyler ditched me for a choir performance at an old folk's center. But the second I step foot into the lunchroom, Max is there. In my face. With a flower? I stop and stare at him.

"Kate. I heard you were sick. And then I heard you were getting better. And then I saw you back in school and I wanted to get you something."

He hands over the limp flower and I wonder where he got it from. Outside? Are there even flowers blooming? Maybe there's an arrangement in the office that's suddenly sparse. "Uh...thanks, Max." Now, *please-leave-me-alone-please-leave-me-alone.*

"Guess I better go get my lunch."

117

I step away and the flower folds over. "Yeah, me too. See ya."

I don't even make it to the lunch line before Charlie stops me. He hasn't talked to me since I told him to leave me alone. Apparently that threat has worn off.

He runs a hand through his hair and cracks his knuckles. "Hey, Kate."

My stomach growls. "What is it, Charlie?"

"Listen. Vivian isn't as bad as you think she is."

Okay? Not what I expected to hear. I'm about to argue the point but I think it would make his speech longer. "Yeah...so?"

"I just wanted to let you know what she really says about you behind your back."

I glance across the room and find Vivian working her flirt charm on Jack. "Look, I really don't care."

"You should." Charlie's boyish eyes soften his outburst. "It will help you see why I hang out with her."

I blink a few times. "You still hang out with her?"

"She's not always bad."

"And being bad is sometimes okay?" I ask.

Charlie shifts his feet. "I overheard her telling someone that you really didn't make out with Jack—"

"Which is true. How does that make her good?"

He waves his hands. "I'm getting there. *Sheesh*. She said she was glad that you told her. I don't think she hates you, Kate. I think she just doesn't know how to make friends."

I try to follow his logic. "You're saying she wants to be my friend?"

Charlie breathes out a puff of air. "I'm saying that she has a bunch of boys as friends because we're the only ones that will give her the time of day."

Apparently she doesn't get along with her twin sister enough to count her as a friend. I cough into my arm and scramble for a good response. "And teasing new kids is going to make them want to be friends with her?"

"Don't you see?" He throws his hands up and I shut my mouth so I can try to *see* something. He's delaying my lunch and I have to do my meds soon. "She doesn't know how to make friends and doesn't know how to get a boyfriend. She likes Jack a lot." Charlie bites his lip and draws his eyebrows together. "It's like this: her whole life she's been fighting for friends with her twin sister. That's the only way she knows how to get attention. To fight for it."

He's finally said something that makes sense. But why I'm having this heart to heart with a boy I've only talked to a couple times is beyond me. "Charlie, why are you telling me this? Do you want me to become friends with her?"

His arms fall. "You don't have to. But don't get mad at me if I am."

I cough again. It's normal. Not like this conversation. "I don't care if you are, but maybe you could help her with the attitude? Deal?"

He looks right at me. "And what about your attitude?"

I flinch. Is that what he's really getting at? Trying to get to the bottom of my personal problems? Another cough cuts off my reply and I wait for it to subside. "You may have Vivian all figured out, but you don't know much about me. Sorry, Charlie."

I turn around and walk away. As much as I want to forget his words, they're like a broken record. *Your attitude. Your attitude. Your attitude.*

Seriously! I can't make it stop. Charlie thinks I'm like Vivian. Sure we both push people away, but I'm not mean about it. Am I? I've been getting better. I'm friends with Giana. And kind of dating Kyler. And what about Mo? Okay, maybe he's only a friend by default since Giana fell for him.

I grab my lunch and head toward the nurse's office. It's not until I'm hooked up to my meds and scarfing down my food in record time that I realize what Charlie's talking about.

I'm trying to let people in.

And Vivian's trying to let people in.

But neither of us really know how.

But how can I? Especially after this most recent infection? As much as I'm prepared for death, I'm more scared now than ever before. And I think it's because I *have* let people in. Giana is a great friend and Kyler...well, he's something else. Something I don't want to think about or it will tear me apart from the inside out—starting with my heart.

My fear isn't so much about them letting me go anymore. If something happens, how will *I* be able to let go?

Chapter 16

I walk into school the next morning and stop right inside the front door. Across the common area, Giana's sitting behind a table with a poster taped to the front that says, *Sign up for the CF walk.*

I stand still and debate whether I should go over or not. This must be her next approach at getting fellow students to care about an uncommon disease. Several kinds walk by, some glance at her poster but most ignore her altogether. Yeah, it's going really well. She's definitely preaching to the wrong crowd.

I push back my annoyance and turn my feet in her direction. In the time it takes me to get there, Mo has laughed twice at something Giana said and now has his hand around the back of her chair. I pause. Maybe it's a bad time to interrupt.

"Hey, Kate." Giana waves at me and I close the distance.

I tilt my head and try not to stare at Mo's hand on her shoulder. Even though the CF awareness campaign may not be going well, their relationship must be on the right path. "Hey,

121

Giana." Yes, I emphasize her name. It's the only way to secretly tell her that I want to know what's going on.

She leans forward, grabs a full-sheet flyer, and hands it to me. "What do you think?"

I scan the info—which lists the basic CF symptoms and walk info at the bottom. "You do realize this is in four months, right?"

She beams and Mo's hand moves forward to tickle her back. My eyebrows shoot up, but she ignores them. "It's never too early to let people know about ways to help a good cause."

I put the paper on top of the stack. "How long are you going to stay out here? Doesn't class start soon?"

She turns to Mo and he checks his cell phone. "Ten minutes," he says.

"I'll wait a couple more minutes and pack up right before class."

I have to think of something to distract me from Mo's sudden interest in Giana. Otherwise, I'm going to ask for more details with him sitting right there. "How's your niece?"

Giana's smile droops a little, but not completely. I can tell she's trying to stay happy about the whole thing. "Good, I guess."

Dang. Mo's got his fingers in Giana's hair.

A cough tickles the back of my throat and makes my eyes water. When it comes out, I struggle to get a good breath. Giana stands up and puts a hand on my back. "Maybe you should get a drink."

I manage to say, "Come with me."

"Okay." She tells Mo she'll be right back. Not that he needs to worry, the drinking fountain is only twenty feet away.

The second I stop drinking, I ask, "Since when did you two become a *thing*?"

Giana turns her head. "Sorry, too close to my bad ear. I didn't hear you."

I repeat the question.

Her face goes red. "We're not really a thing."

I give her a funny look and shake my head. "Yes, you are."

She giggles. "So, maybe he does like me a little."

I lift an eyebrow. "Sure. Just a little."

She touches my arm. "What about you and Kyler?"

"What about us?"

"Tammy told me she heard from Lily that you two were holding hands in the hallway."

Of course Lily would know about it. Vivian probably told her. My cheeks suddenly feel flushed and Giana's bouncing on her toes again.

"I knew your date went better than you said. You like him right?"

Now my cheeks are burning. "Of course I do. Why else would we be holding hands?"

"I'm so excited for you two. Did you tell him about your CF yet?"

Her question kills my excitement. Short answer: no. Long answer: I haven't said anything because I'm afraid it will scare him away. I bite my lip and shake my head.

Giana calms down. "It's okay, Kate. I was just curious." She touches my arm again. "But I think he'd understand. Kyler's really a great guy."

I groan. "I know he is. And that's why I don't want to tell him. I don't want to lose him."

123

Her eyebrows pull together. "You won't. Only an idiot would let that bother them."

Right?

"Giana," Mo calls across the commons area. "It's time to pack up."

"Guess I better go," she says.

I nod. "Yeah, me too."

When I get to psychology, Kyler's already sitting in his chair. He turns around and winks at me as the teacher starts class.

My conversation with Giana makes me wonder what Kyler would really do if he found out. He's gone through some hard things, so maybe he'd understand. But what if he doesn't want to be with me *because* he's gone through something so hard before? I'd have to tell him that there's a possibility that I'll die, and the thought of him losing someone else crumbles my heart.

Maybe I should just break things off with him.

I gaze at his back and tune out everything else—everything but the pounding against my ribs and the soft sound of his voice in my mind. It pulls at my emotions and fills me with hope. I try to remember what kept me going before I met him, but it doesn't work. It's *his* hand that leads me down French streets. His voice that erases pain better than most medication. His attention that makes me feel like a priceless work of art.

No. I can't push him away. I'll tell him about my cystic fibrosis, and if he decides he doesn't want to be with me, at least I can hold onto his memories. Without them, I might drown in the constant battle to stay alive.

A tear escapes through my closed eyelids and I rub it away with my palm. I press my eyes, pushing back any more tears that might reveal my secrets. It doesn't work. I sniff hard and it comes out as a terrible cough. I open my eyes and find Kyler watching me as I cry, cough, and plan to tell him something that just might scare him away.

I jump from my seat and rush to the bathroom. Only then do I let the tears flow. Each time I gasp for air, another cough joins the battle. Back and forth. It's like I'm grieving for a lifetime of sickness in this one moment. I'm loud and sick and when I finally settle down, I'm a mess. Even if Kyler doesn't leave me because of my disease, my new look will scare him away in a second.

I'll tell him tomorrow. Today, I'm going home. My throat aches, my stomach hurts, and there's a throbbing in my chest that's turning my brain to mush. I can't learn anything like this. Besides, it will take all day to prepare me for my confession in the morning.

Giana's right. Kyler should know.

Chapter 17

The first thing on my mind in the morning is Kyler. I'm telling Kyler about my CF today. Even though I'm still not ready, it's time. I want him to like me for *all* of me.

I breathe in and cough out. That's how my mornings go, but this is different...something's not right. I open my eyes and it's dark. One look at the glowing clock confirms that it's not morning. Why am I awake at four thirty? I turn onto my back and gasp from a sharp pain on my right side. My sudden intake of air makes me curl in a ball, coughing until my vision gets blurry.

I can't move.

I can't breathe.

I can't stop coughing.

I struggle out of bed and crawl across my room to get my inhaler. It shakes between my trembling fingers, but I get a good hold on it and breathe in a dose of meds. The pain in my back pierces through my body and there's a deep ache in my chest.

I fall to the floor and cry out. Seconds later, the door swings open and Mom enters. Her eyes scan my bed and she finally finds me.

"Kate," she gasps. Her face turns to stone as she dashes across my room to kneel beside me.

A moan curdles in my throat.

"Where does it hurt?" she asks in a flat voice. Even though her questions are calculated and monotone, her hands are gentle on my face.

"My back."

"Your back? Maybe you have a rib out."

I cough so hard it brings up yucky stuff and Mom grabs a tissue. Behind her rigid eyes, there's a shred of panic.

"Does it hurt anywhere else?" she asks quickly.

I pat my chest and try for another deep breath. It hurts too bad. Tears sting my eyes and I fight them down. Another crying episode might result in one cough too many. It's hard to talk, but I need to explain everything to my mom. "It's...hard...to breathe." Long exhale.

Mom grabs my pillow and lightly rests my head on top. "I'm getting my keys and we're going to the hospital. Do you think you can walk?"

"No."

Mom runs out of the room and returns in a minute. Somehow she's dressed with shoes on and a purse over her shoulder. "I'm going to help you to the car. Stay with me, okay?"

Sure. Stay with her; don't let the pain take over my thoughts completely. Mom picks me up and slides a hand under my armpits. Most of my weight is on her, but I do my best to move my feet down the hall, out the door, and into the car. Mom sinks behind the wheel and we're off to the hospital.

The hospital. My brain starts to shut off but Mom said to stay with her. If I zone out, it might be too hard to tune back in. Instead I close my eyes and curl into a ball, still coughing and still struggling to take each breath. But I do, in and out, in and out. It helps to focus on that one thing.

"We're here," Mom finally says.

I don't move until she has my door open. She calls out for a wheelchair and places a hand on my arm.

"It's going to be okay, Kate. Everything will be okay."

That's what we always say. And it's always been true, but this time I'm not sure it's going to work out. I'm hoping for the best, but it seems impossible when the worst is staring me right in the face. As much as I try not to tune out, the only way my mind can handle everything is to mush it all together. If I focus too much on one thing, it might consume me completely. I'm wheeled into triage where they take my stats and do a few oxygen tests. When the nurse tries to listen to my lungs, his face pulls into a sudden frown.

He opens his mouth and my hands tighten around the armrests. I close my eyes for the bad news.

"We need to get an x-ray of her lungs right away."

I'm moving, going down one hall and into another. The nurse pushes me fast and Mom has to hurry to keep up. Her hard features have turned into angled lines. Worried, tired, set on getting me better. They wheel me right into an x-ray room and move me to the table. It's hard to get a good picture since I'm coughing so much. But once the task is done, I'm wheeled into a hospital room and moved to a bed.

The nurse questions my mom while he hooks me up with some oxygen. He starts an IV and tells Mom that they're giving me pain medication for my back and chest.

"We've called Doctor Perry," the nurse says. "He should be here in a few minutes. Once he arrives, he'll look at the x-rays and take things from there."

The second he leaves, Mom comes to my side. Her hard outer shell is gone. A tear rolls down her cheek and she wipes it away with the back of her hand. "I'm so sorry, honey. I know how much you hate being here."

I stare at her and blink through the first wave of pain-killer haze. It's taking over my words and making my eyelids droop.

Mom sniffles. "Get some rest, Kate."

I close my eyes, but I can't clear my mind. A thought keeps me awake: I never got to tell Kyler about my disease. Now I may never get the chance.

Doc Perry walks in. My eyelids are heavy but I manage to keep them open. Doc's standing at the wall in front of an x-ray reader. When he steps back, I see the x-ray of my lungs. They don't look right. The two sides don't match. Doc glances at me and nods. He knows I can tell something's wrong.

"Your right lung is seventy percent collapsed," he says.

I can't decide whether I should mourn the seventy percent or be happy that I still have the other thirty. Without it, I would have been dead by now.

"We're going to insert a chest tube to remove the air and fluid that have taken over the empty space."

There's a knock at the door and Doc Perry lets in the nurse with a tray. Of all the things on it, the one that catches my eye is a big needle. Huge. It makes my stomach tighten and my hands tremble. Now? Aren't they going to numb me first? The nurse sets the tray next to my bed and Doc steps closer. He pulls down the top of my gown and feels around my chest.

His finger stops and he says, "Here."

The nurse hands him the needle and he doesn't even tell me it's going to hurt. I know it is. I just hope the pain meds in my IV will help. The needle goes in and I try to scream. My brain is shutting down. I'm losing consciousness. I can't do this. I can't think. There's only pain.

Deep.

Sharp.

Pain.

It pierces my chest and radiates outward. A slight pressure on my hand diverts my attention. I try to move my fingers but someone's squeezing them. It must be Mom and she must be trying to keep me here. Just like she said. "Stay with me."

I fight against the pain with every last ounce of energy. Sweat trickles down my forehead and leaves a cool path behind. Think about cool, think about sweat, think about…anything but the pain. The pressure lets up and I barely lift an eyelid. The needle is sticking out of my chest and Doc's putting a tiny tube into it. Down it goes, into my body. And then it's done, the needle comes out and the tube is attached to a suction that does all the work.

They clean up and turn to my mom to discuss details. I ease into a distant place. One without extra therapy, meds, or visits. They'll come when they need to come and I'll be here, tied to the bed by a twelve foot tube. I stare at the ceiling and grasp for a happy thought.

Kyler…

No, I can't think about him without feeling bad that I never shared my biggest secret. He told me of his mother's death and instead of trusting him with mine, I kept it to myself. Now he might not ever find out from me. I clench my fists and sort through my brain for a different kind of distraction.

Darts. I need my darts and target. I need something...anything to channel my anger before the blank walls and tinted windows drive me crazy. The specks on the ceiling mesh together and the muffled conversation between Doc Perry and Mom slips away. They must've put something in my IV. It's the only explanation behind my sudden stillness. I can't hold on much longer. Mom said to stay with her, but it's impossible. We've hit the worst and now we just need to hope for the best.

Before the meds take over completely, I find the voice that lulls me into a calm trance. I can't fight thoughts of Kyler now. He may never know the hope and peace his clear, smooth voice brings me. My anger from earlier disappears and leaves his image in my mind. His freckles, boyish curls, and soft words take over my thoughts. I let the music fill my head and fall into a quiet slumber.

* * *

I wake up to the familiar speckled ceiling. A whiteboard across the room has a series of times and meds recorded in black marker. Up in the right corner is the name of my nurse. Ember. I think it's a female name, but I'm not certain. When the door opens and a strange woman walks in, all doubts wash away.

"Alrighty," she says after washing her hands. "Time for your meds."

"How long have I been asleep?"

She shrugs. "Only a few hours, but I'm glad you're awake."

I lift an eyebrow. She's probably only glad because it gives her one less thing to worry about.

She continues, "And we need to order some food. It's almost time to switch your IV as well. If we get it all finished, you'll have time to rest again."

After the list she just recited, I'm not sure I'm going to get *any* rest. "Where's my mom?"

Ember exchanges my IV bags and turns to me. "She had to get to work but she'll be by as soon as she's off."

Awesome. Now I'm on a strict schedule in a place that smells like iodine and I get to share all my time with Ember. Not that I don't like her...I just don't like being here. We start my meds, run some tests, and then I eat. Lots of food. Since my body doesn't absorb it well, it takes a lot of calories to keep my energy up. Even after a full meal, I'm exhausted. I fall back to sleep until Ember wakes me up to do it all again.

Every day.

In that room.

Mom stops by as often as she can, but the days drag on. I spend my time watching mindless television shows and imagining different ways to get out of the hospital. Not realistic ones, of course: ones that use karate moves and sleeping darts. It's pointless, but it helps.

One night, Mom comes right after I finish my dinner. My stomach hurts and I hate eating so much, but I have to.

"Hey, honey." Mom flings her purse on the couch and comes right to my bed. "How's my favorite girl?"

I smile. She has asked me the same question during every hospital visit since I could remember. "I need something to keep my mind off of..." I can't say the next words, but I don't have to. Mom already knows.

"That's why I brought you this." She pulls out a stack of DVDs and sets them on my table.

"What are they?"

"You don't know this, but I filmed almost every one of your karate lessons."

I tilt my head. "What about the ones you were teaching?"

"Bob filmed those."

He's the manager of the studio. I slide my hand over a DVD case, the smooth plastic slick beneath my fingers. This could be good...or really bad. I never got my black belt, but I could fend for myself in a one-on-one fight. My first lesson was right after Mom told Dad I was dead.

I swallow and narrow my eyes on Mom. "Can I ask you something?"

"Always."

My heart pulses and I scratch my face under the oxygen tube. "Why did you tell Dad that I was dead?"

Mom's face hardens and her jaw twitches. I'm sure she didn't expect that question but it's something I've thought about off and on since she shut the door in his face. I didn't dare ask her before but now it feels right. Besides, there might not be much time left for her to answer anything.

At first I don't think she's going to answer. She rubs her hands across her lap and takes a deep breath. "He made his choice when he left the first time, Kate. I didn't want him to walk out again."

"But how do you know he would? You never gave him the chance." Not that I did either. I just sat there when he was standing ten feet away. Sometimes I wish I'd done something to let him know I was actually there.

Her lips press together and she closes her eyes. "You don't know him the way I did. We were together five years before I even got pregnant with you. He was in and out of the relationship all the time. I thought he would change after we got married but when he left, I knew he'd never come back. Not for real. I needed him to be gone...for the both of us."

I bite my quivering lip. Having him around sometimes might have been better than never. I have no idea what it's like to have a father. No uncles, grandfathers, nothing. Just doctors who want to know how much I weigh and how much oxygen I have in my body.

Mom puts her head down and pinches the bridge of her nose. I rub my eyes and let thoughts of Dad melt away. Of course there's no dad that could replace the love of my mom. And right now, she needs me just as much as I need her. I put a hand on her shoulder and she lifts her face. Tears stream down her cheeks and I pull her into an awkward hug.

I hold her close and let her tears land on my shoulder. "I'm lucky to have you."

She backs away and wipes her face with a tissue. "I'm sorry." We sit there for a minute more while the silence eases the tension. Mom grabs a DVD and sticks it in the machine. "Let's check out those mad skills."

I laugh. "Mine or yours?"

She doesn't answer, just settles on the couch with a light blue hospital blanket. As long as I stare at the screen, I can imagine I'm back at home. No tubes, no monitors, no IVs.

134

Just me and my mom watching a show and enjoying a night together.

Chapter 18

The next afternoon, I get a new visitor. Giana walks in the door as my nurse is leaving.

"Wash your hands, please, and don't get too close," Ember says.

Giana washes her hands for a good minute, soaping twice, then sits on the edge of the couch, near me. "I'm sorry, I would've come sooner, but they wouldn't let me. How do you feel?"

I can't help laughing. It's like the number one conversation starter and also the worst thing to ask someone with multiple tubes in their body. "Crappy." No, I'm not going to lie.

Giana presses her lips together and relaxes into the couch.

"Have you had any luck with donations for the CF walk?" I ask.

She shakes her head and pauses with a mysterious curve to her lips. "No, but guess what? Mo kissed me last night."

My jaw drops. I snap it shut and say, "Spill."

"Well...he came over for *homework*."

I laugh. "Yeah right."

"We really did do homework. But afterwards, I walked him out to his car and he leaned in for a kiss. I just couldn't leave him hangin'." Her eyes light up and her lips are curved into a huge smile.

"Right. You two probably made out."

She giggles. "No. It was just a few kisses."

I lift an eyebrow.

"I'm serious. And I would've told you last night," she says. "But you never answer your phone."

I raise my empty hands. "It's not allowed. Mom won't let me have a phone in the hospital anyway. She says it takes away from rest time. If she were here long enough, she'd realize that the nurses do a good enough job of that already."

"How are your lungs?" Giana asks.

I shrug. "This morning they were a little better. I still can't get up much, but they want me to start physical therapy soon."

"Is that possible?"

"Only after my fluid levels go down. Right now, I'm connected to the building." I point to the tubes running from me to the wall.

Giana shifts in her seat and clears her throat. "I brought you some magazines."

I'm reluctant to celebrate the fact. "Please don't tell me they're for teens."

She reaches in her bag and pulls out a stack of tattered magazines. "Nope. I found these old European architecture magazines online."

"Did they cost you a fortune?"

Giana shakes her head. "Actually, someone was getting rid of them for free."

"Seriously, how do you *find* these things?"

She sets them next to my karate DVDs and stands near the bed. "Have you talked to Kyler?" she asks.

Kyler. Of course she had to bring him up. I've been thinking about him nonstop until she walked in the door. "No. He still doesn't know either."

"Do you want him to?"

I clench my fists. "Yes. I mean, I was going to tell him...but this all happened."

"You know, you do have a *hospital* phone."

My shoulders slump forward. "I know, but I can't tell him over the phone. I've ran it through my head several times and it just wouldn't be the same."

Giana folds her arms. "Well, I guess that's true." After a few seconds, she snaps her fingers. "Listen, I gotta run but I'll come visit you again when I can."

"You're leaving already?"

Her lips pull down in a frown. "I'm sorry. My mom wants me home to help with dinner. I told her you're here but she didn't want to know any details."

"Still having a hard time with it all?" I ask.

"You have no idea. I promise to come back before you get released." She waves goodbye and walks out.

The second Giana's gone, I realize how much I've missed having her around. Not just her, but everyone. Even though I don't have a lot of friends, there's something comforting about knowing Mo will be next to Giana, Max will be in my face, Vivian will be...well, Vivian with Charlie, and Kyler will be—

What will Kyler be? Hanging out with his choir buddies? Singing melodies to someone else? It kills me that I haven't heard from him. Does he even miss me? I know what Mom would say. If he doesn't stick around, he wasn't worth my time in the first place. Yada-yada-yada...

But Kyler *isn't* like my dad. At least, I hope he isn't.

I don't have to wait long to find out. When I wake from my afternoon nap the next day, Kyler's leaning against the wall near my door. His knee is bent with his foot flat on the wall and a bouquet of flowers hanging from his fist.

I sit up and rub my eyes to make sure he's really there. My gown falls off one shoulder and I hurry to pull it back up. My neck grows hot and I clear my throat. "Hi."

Kyler's foot thumps to the floor and he steps closer. "Hi."

"You're here."

He lifts the flowers. "I'm here."

The echo response has to stop. "How did you find me?"

He shrugs. "Giana."

She did seem a little excited to leave yesterday. Maybe this was her big plan. Well, it's definitely making me cross the bridge I was stuck on. "Do you want to sit down?" And look at the tubes, and see my fluids, and listen to me cough? It's like I'm asking him to enjoy a nice stay in a torture chamber.

He sits and leans forward. "Why didn't you tell me you were this sick?" He rubs a hand over his forehead and closes his eyes. "I mean, you just left class and never came back. Then I found out you went home. I couldn't even get a hold of you. Then Giana tells me days later that you're in the hospital?"

I swallow and blink. Then swallow and blink again. Where to start? "I'm sorry I didn't tell you. I was going to."

He looks up and his jaw twitches. "You planned on telling me you were sick enough to go to the hospital?"

The rough tone in his voice weakens my courage. "No, Kyler." He drops his hands. "I was planning on telling you about my lifelong disease."

He flinches. "Wait, what? Giana didn't say anything about—"

"Of course she didn't. Because it's my secret to tell." My throat goes dry and I cough. "I have cystic fibrosis."

His face falls and I can see our connection dying. This is it. Kyler isn't going to want me anymore. He's going to get up and tell me that he can't handle something like that right now. His mouth opens and he says, "Why does that sound so familiar?"

I try to calm my racing heart enough to focus on his question. "Because. Giana's been spreading awareness for the last week."

"You have that same disease?"

I nod. "That's why I cough. That's why I get sick. And *that's* why I'm in the hospital."

"But are you okay?"

I lift an eyebrow and my hands wave around the room. "I guess you can call this okay. I'm alive."

"So you're not dying?" His voice is hopeful, beautiful.

My arms tingle and I smile. "I'm not planning on it. At least not yet." Not that I ever plan on it, but eventually it will happen. Kyler sighs and sinks into the couch while I think of something else to talk about. "How's school?" I ask.

He gives a slight chuckle. "You've missed some weird stuff in psychology."

"Not really. My mom brings me my schoolwork."

He looks at me. "I'm not sure about all those complexes."

I shrug. "Then don't worry about them. It's only a basic overview of disproved theories. Just because something's backed by studies doesn't mean it will always happen. It only takes one person to bring about change." I think of Giana and her efforts in finding a cure for CFers. She probably won't find one, but because she's spreading awareness, Kyler already knows a few things about the disease. Every little bit helps.

Silence falls between us and I focus on the steady hum from my equipment. What else should I say to Kyler? It's hard to think about anything but my disease when the whole room's filled with evidence of its destruction.

Kyler bumps the remote and my ten-year-old self pops up on the screen, chopping a piece of wood in two with my hand.

"Whoa," Kyler says. He looks at me then back at the screen. "Is that you?"

"Yes."

He turns to me with a smug look. "You like to sit around and watch how good you are, don't you?"

I laugh. "Maybe."

"Dang. You're good *and* conceited. No wonder Charlie's afraid of you."

Charlie. He thinks I'm just like Vivian. I don't want people to be afraid of me, but I may never get a chance to show him that I'm not really like that. Everything in my life revolves around my sicknesses. It's always about me. I don't want to be this way.

I glance at the screen. My ten-year-old self does a roundhouse kick and it triggers a cough attack. Mom's at my side, her face hard and her hand on my back. She gets me a drink and pushes me to try again. She shows me the way it's done and I follow.

"Is that your mom?" Kyler asks.

"Yeah."

He looks away from the screen and his gaze roams over my face. "Remind me not to get on her bad side." His words float in my ear and I swallow the sudden knot in my throat. We stare at each other and the room grows small. I breathe in and he breathes out. We're close but still too far away. I want to reach out and touch him but I'm not sure if I should. He just holds my gaze.

I wish I knew what's going through his head. Is he scared of the real me or is he okay with it? What's he thinking?

"Kate." His voice is soft.

My knees tremble and I almost forget that I'm in the hospital. The way he says my name takes me far away: to a moonlit night, or walking across a bridge hand in hand. That's where we should be. Not here in this germ-infested building.

I curse the tubes and focus on Kyler. He gives me hope of somewhere special and that's exactly what I need. I need to know that there's something worth living for. That if I ever get out of this place, there will be people at my side—people like my mom and Giana. And maybe even Kyler.

He gets up and inches toward the bed. His mouth lifts on one side and he laughs. "When you get out of here, you'll have to teach me to fight like your mom."

"What?" I'm so shocked, I lose track of my thoughts.

"You don't want to learn to fight like me? Am I not good enough?"

"Oh, you're good enough. But if I'm going to beat you, I have to be better."

I'm laughing and coughing and practically blowing snot all over the place. I grab a tissue and bury my face to hide the grossness. But I can't stop laughing.

I feel a hand on my foot and Kyler says, "I'm sorry, Kate. I didn't mean to make you cry."

I snort back another laugh and it brings on more giggles. He thinks I'm crying. If I don't stop, I *will* be crying. Happy tears. Somehow I manage to lift my face.

Kyler looks confused.

I rub my nose. "How about I'll teach you how to fight like my mom if you teach me how to sing like your dad?"

Kyler finally sees that I'm still laughing. He joins in and holds my foot tighter. "My dad can't even sing."

I shrug and gain some control over my giggles. The air between us grows still and his tense expression is back. A thought crosses my mind and races out my mouth. "I'll teach you to fight like my mom if you teach me to sing like yours did."

The laughter is gone now. I hope I didn't say the wrong thing. Kyler's eyes are on me but they're distant. I bite my lip and wait for him to respond.

He wiggles my foot and clears his throat. "I better go. I'll be back tomorrow though."

143

"Really?"

He smiles. "I gotta start learning those skills sometime." He points to the stack of DVDs. "Looks like you've had the best lessons in town."

He lets go of my foot and it feels cold. "Thanks for coming by, Kyler."

"I wish you would've told me sooner," he whispers. I barely hear him but his comment hits me with a blast of guilt.

"I know," I say softly. "But thanks for understanding."

He folds his arms and pierces me with his gaze. "Sometimes it only takes one person who understands to make a difference. Everyone knows about my mom, but no one really knew the right things to say. What I needed was for someone to say nothing—to be themselves around me because I'm me. My mom's death made everyone act different, but you didn't know about it. And even after I told you, you treated me the same. If anyone should be thankful, it's me."

He pauses for a deep breath. I hold still, cherishing this moment before it's even over.

"I wish I could teach you to sing like my mom, but her voice was like an angel's. And as much as I'd like to hear her again, I'm not sure I'm ready for that yet."

I open my mouth to respond, but Kyler's already on his way out the door. Before leaving, he gives me one last grin and a small wave of his hand. I hold onto his words and feel better than I have since I entered the hospital. Kyler made me feel like I was living, breathing on my own, released from this glorified prison to a happier place.

Now I know for certain why Mom had me make friends—because I literally couldn't live without them. They help me feel alive and give me a reason to fight. I would've fought to stay alive with Mom, but it's like each person who cares is another person worth living for. I've always heard the phrase "the more the merrier," but I never believed it until now.

I will live for Mom.

I will live for Giana and Kyler.

I will live for Max and Vivian.

And I will live every day for everyone else who wants to be a part of my life.

I will live and I will breathe.

Chapter 19

When Kyler walks in the next day, he's carrying a strange instrument case. Almost like a guitar but circular. I know I've seen something like it before, but I can't seem to remember its name.

"What's that?" I ask as he sits on the couch and lays it across his lap.

"A banjo."

Right. I knew that. Now I just look dumb. "Please tell me you know how to play it."

"No. I only brought it to give you something else to stare at."

I arch an eyebrow as high as it will go and tilt my head. "Really?"

Kyler laughs and flips the case open. "You're so gullible, Kate."

"What? How was I supposed to know you played that? You've never said anything about it before."

His lip quirks up on one side. "You're not the only one who can keep a secret." Kyler pulls the banjo out and sets the case on the cushion beside him. He holds the instrument like it's a part of his body.

"Is it hard to play?" I ask.

Kyler places his fingers on the strings and strums a chord with the other hand. A *twang* fills the air and goose bumps flare along my arms.

"It was really hard to learn at first," he says. "But I'm glad I stuck with it."

"What made you want to learn?" I ask. There was a time I considered learning the guitar, but I think everyone's tempted by that at least once. Seriously, who doesn't look hotter playing a guitar? I never imagined myself playing the banjo, though. That's like saying it would be nice to learn how to play the accordion. I thought it was an old-fashioned thing to do.

But Kyler definitely doesn't look old. In fact, if anyone else knew how hot he looked with that thing across his lap, they'd want to learn how to play it as well.

Kyler strums a few notes and lets the music hang in the air before he mutes it with his hand. He looks up and shrugs. "When I was little, a bluegrass group came into town. One of the band members picked up a banjo and stood at the mic to sing a solo while he played. I decided right then that I wanted to be able to do that one day."

"Is today that day?" Please say yes.

"No. Today's the day we play a game. You know some music, right?"

I almost laugh. "Not much, really."

"I'll go easy on you. I'm going to play a song and you guess what it is."

I stare at him. Hard. "Maybe no one has told you I'm tone deaf."

147

Kyler grips the banjo handle and winks at me. "Don't worry. A two year old could guess these songs."

I take a deep breath and cough a few times. Once I've recovered, Kyler plinks out a few notes on the banjo.

It takes all of three seconds to realize what he's playing. "Row, Row, Row Your Boat?"

He lifts a hand. "See? Told you it would be easy."

"You're just lucky I went to girl scouts a handful of times when I was little."

"No, you're the lucky one."

"Really?"

Kyler changes his fingers to a different chord. "Yes. Otherwise *I* would be winning this game."

I clasp my hands together and let my head sink into the pillow. "Okay. I'm ready for the next one. You're totally going down by the way."

Kyler plays another song and I guess what it is. *Twinkle Twinkle Little Star*. I don't know the one after that, but in the end, I win most of the rounds.

Kyler sets his banjo on top of the case and puts his elbows on his knees, leaning closer to me. "Told you I'd go easy on you."

I laugh and it triggers another cough. "Aren't you going to play me something real?"

"I think you just offended someone in their grave. Don't you know those *are* real songs?"

I try to swat Kyler but I can't reach his arm. "Seriously."

"Seriously? Yes. I am going to play you something real. But only after you perfect at least *one* chord."

I blink. "You've got to be kidding."

Kyler lifts his hands. "I never kid."

"Oh man. Okay. Give it to me so we can get this over with." He's going to regret trying to teach me anything. Especially with so many tubes coming out of my body. This could take all night.

On second thought. I like this plan. Kyler sets the banjo on my lap—

"Wait."

He freezes.

"We really should sanitize it first. Who knows what you've touched before playing this. No offense."

Kyler hesitates, then says, "Of course. Where are the wipes?"

After we get the banjo all cleaned, I hold it in my hands. The wood is smooth under my fingers and the strings are tight. "Okay, wise guy, what do I do?"

Kyler explains where my fingers go. After a few minutes, I give him a flat look. "Isn't there an easy chord with only one string to push down?"

He doesn't look at me. "Not the one I'm teaching you."

I strum a note and cringe as the sound grates my eardrums.

"Okay," Kyler says. "That was nice if you were playing for a haunted house."

I lean over with a laugh and my fingers fall out of place. "Please teach me something simpler."

"You know, sometimes the best things in life take the most work."

I pause. He couldn't have described my life any better. Everything I've done has taken work. Each breath I take is

149

harder for me than the average person. And I'd do it over and over again just to stay alive—to live in this moment and continue doing hard things.

I place my fingers back on the strings and try to remember where they're supposed to be. "Okay, teach me this difficult chord."

It takes nearly five minutes just to get my hands in the right place. By the time we do, my small fingers are bent funny and there's an ache running up my arm.

"I think you're ready," Kyler says. "Go ahead and strum your other fingers along the strings."

Sweat trickles down the back of my neck. I close my eyes and play the chord. The sound vibrates into the instrument and echoes through the room. It floats in my ear and seeps through my body like a warm summer afternoon.

"Wow," I say.

"I know, right? Good job. You finally got it."

I open my eyes and hand over the banjo. "Your turn."

Kyler takes the instrument and attaches it to his body. And even though he doesn't sing, the music has the same effect as his voice. I lean into my pillow and think of Paris.

When the song ends, I tell him, "Thanks."

"For what?"

"For sharing that with me."

"I thought you hated learning that one chord."

I sigh. "I did. But it was worth it so I could listen to all the others."

Kyler packs up and walks across the room. "I have to go, but I'll see you tomorrow." He offers a short nod and leaves.

Chapter 20

Kyler visits almost every day. He comes after school and leaves right before dinner. My nurse has made it a point to get everything done before he gets there and resume everything after. I promise her to rest as much as I can in between everything else. It's a good routine.

Kyler and I don't talk about his mom or my disease; just go on like there aren't multiple tubes in my body and oxygen in my nose. We watch several of my karate tapes together. Today he brings pizza—which means he can stay a little bit longer since we'll be eating dinner together.

The nurse gives me my enzymes and a new cup of water. I put them in my mouth and swallow.

"I think I've seen you take those before," Kyler says.

I shrug. All my previous concerns seem silly now. "Probably. I tried to hide it, but Vivian saw it the first day."

Kyler chuckles. "Only because she was watching you like a hawk."

True. But I don't want to talk about her. "How are things at school?"

"Normal. Boring. I actually look forward to coming to the hospital every day."

I wait to bite the pizza halfway to my mouth. "Am I supposed to be offended by that?"

"What? No." Kyler wipes his lips. "It's just..." His hands twist around each other. "I've avoided hospitals since my mom died."

Of course. And now we've broken our silent agreement. We talked about my pills—which is basically part of my disease—and he just brought up his mom.

"Wait," I say, coming up with a way to get past the uncomfortable lull. "I'm in a hospital?" I put my pizza down and do a fake surprised glance around me. "Who put these tubes in my body?"

Kyler points to himself and shakes his head. "Not me."

We eat the rest of dinner in silence then Kyler goes off about some funny thing that happened with pizza after a choir performance. I'm too busy listening to his voice to pay attention to the details. Honestly, his mom *had* to sound angelic if her voice was any better than his.

Kyler pauses and I ask, "Will you sing me something?"

He shuts his mouth quickly and shrugs. "Sure. I guess. What do you want to hear?"

Anything. "Do you know any songs in French?"

He shakes his head. It was worth a shot.

"I do know an Italian song, though."

I smile. "Is it the one you sang at the assembly?"

"Yes. It might not sound as good because it's really a two part, but I can try."

Knowing anything would sound good coming out of Kyler's mouth, I settle into my pillows and close my eyes.

"You don't want to watch me sing?" he asks.

152

I open my eyes to see his arched brows. "It's easier to pretend I'm not in a hospital if I can't see anything." And I really want to picture us in the French Riviera...so I close my eyes again.

"Okay. Here goes."

Kyler takes a deep breath and his voice comes out like sweet cream. It's soft in my ears and smooth along my skin. I drink it in and paint the perfect picture of his arms around me. He's singing in my ear, whispering a prescription I can't buy at a store. I sink further into the pillows and let the surge of adrenaline rush through me. My body is healing and my heart is growing. Kyler's song melts my worries and lifts me high above the ground where I find a tower of hope. It's held together with music notes and stolen breaths. And right on top, I imagine Kyler embracing me, his finger trailing the edge of my jaw. He lifts my chin ever so slightly and leans forward. I'm falling into him, pressing against the stones beneath my feet to reach his lips.

The song ends and I squeeze my eyes tighter, grasping onto the drifting pieces of a kiss that never happened, and can't happen for some time. Why is the song over? Why am I stuck in a bed? And why can't I *really* hold onto Kyler?

"Kate, are you okay?"

No? Yes...I open my eyes and find Kyler sitting closer than he has before. Every time he's visited, he's kept his distance. But now I can smell his cologne, feel his warmth, and see the tiny freckle on his lips. I blink and look away. I can't think about his lips. It leaves me cold and mad and wanting. Wanting to get out of this hospital and mad that I'm not better yet.

"I'm okay." I swallow. "Thank you for singing that song. Your voice is something else."

Kyler's eyebrows rise. "Is that a good thing or bad?"

That's debatable. Bad because it makes me think of things I can't have. But I don't tell him about that. "Good. *Really* good."

"I gotta get going," Kyler says, but he doesn't move. He leans closer and his hand inches toward mine.

I freeze.

His fingers twitch as I reach mine forward.

When they touch, fire shoots up my arm and ignites my whole body. The flames rage through my limbs as Kyler lets go and stands.

"I'll see you tomorrow," he says.

All I can manage is a small nod. My words turn to smoke and my heart burns deep inside me.

When Mom shows up a half hour later, my cheeks are still warm.

"How's my favorite girl?" she asks.

I sigh. "Good."

Mom sets her purse down and turns to me. "Kyler was here, wasn't he?"

"Yes, Mom."

Her eyebrows angle in a pre-lecture kind of way.

I put my hands up to stop her verbal kick-punch. "Don't worry. Nothing happened. How can it?"

She opens her mouth then shuts it. A few seconds later she says, "You're right. Besides, Ember would do more damage than I could if she knew he was too close."

I'm still not sure if she's worried about the germs or about him being alone with me in a room...even though I'm a network of tubes and monitors. Yeah, that's all kinds of romantic.

"How was work?" I ask.

"Fine. I brought you something."

"More videos?"

Mom reaches into her purse and pulls out a bundle of darts that are missing the sharp points. "I couldn't bring the board because they won't let you throw them, but they said any hobby reminders would be better than nothing."

She puts one in my hand and I roll it between my fingers. The movement is nostalgic. It's always been a way for me to channel my anger and release it in an instant. But right now I'm not angry. I set the dart on my side table. "Thanks."

Mom sits down and rests her elbows on her knees. "What did Doc Perry say this morning?"

"I'm getting better. If my fluid levels lower enough by morning, they'll attach me to a smaller portable pump. Which means..."

"You'll get to start physical therapy?" Her eyes light up.

I glance at the dart. "No, it means I can get out of this room."

Her stern expression returns. "To do physical therapy."

"I'd like to think my whole life doesn't revolve around medical terms."

"I'm glad you're getting better. Just wait. You'll be back home in no time."

Home. It seems like a nice dream. Hopefully soon, it will be reality.

* * *

155

I'm doing much better by morning. I'm hooked up to a smaller tube that connects to a portable pump. The physical therapist comes in and explains what he wants me to do to get my body and lungs working more. Laps. At least once a day around my hospital wing but twice would be better. I can almost feel the freedom, and the pain.

What if the pain comes back?

Giana comes during lunch and walks with me for my first time around. It's nice to have her there so I don't think about how slow we're really going. We go around, step by step, second by second. She talks about Mo and I push the wheelchair that holds my pump. Halfway around, I have to sit down to rest. Then we keep going.

By the next day, I can do the whole thing without stopping. Kyler walks beside me this time and hums the Italian song. It pushes me on and helps me float back to my room.

I'm getting better and I know it's because I have people who care. Even if they can't find a cure, it's comforting to know they accept me for who I am and want the best for me.

After a week of physical therapy, my oxygen levels are better, my tubes are out, and I finally get to go home.

Chapter 21

I can't go back to school yet, but Mom lets me sit on the front porch. I wrap up in a blanket and listen to the sounds of laughter coming from the park. The air smells like fresh rain with a hint of garlic from someone's dinner. I breathe it in and snuggle deeper into the fabric surrounding me. A man and woman walk by, led by two huskies on leashes. They wave and I smile.

This may be a new home with unfamiliar neighbors, but it's home. A soft breeze tickles the top of my head and a white SUV drives past. I stare at the worn asphalt and listen to the rocks crunch as the vehicle moves farther away. Clouds layer the sky above me: gray and white, with every shade in between. Pockets of blue sky peek through, but the sun stays hidden.

I soak it in and vow never to go back inside, even though I know it's not realistic. Visions of the hospital swirl through my mind and I shudder. No more needles, no more nurses...no more secrets. Kyler finally knows about my CF and he still hasn't run away.

I pull out my phone and text him to see when he'll be by.

A minute later, a figure in a blue puffy coat cruises down the sidewalk on a longboard. They're about to pass me when they jump off instead and let the board crash into my mailbox.

I lean forward to stand, but I'm too slow. The person lifts their face and I cringe.

"Vivian?"

She glances down the street. "I didn't know you lived here."

I press my lips together, still shocked to see her on my front lawn.

"You look like…" Her gaze scrutinizes my face and trails down the blanket.

"Crap?" I ask.

Her eyes grow. "I wasn't going to say it."

"You don't have to, Vivian. It was probably something worse anyway." My body sinks into the cement and I suddenly wish I'd stayed inside. This isn't the break I was hoping for.

She folds her arms. "Where have you been?"

Really? Like I'd tell her. The only thing she's ever wanted from me is trouble. Except, now all I can think about are Charlie's words. She wants friends. And I want friends. But that doesn't mean I choose *her* as a friend. I rub my temples and try to come up with a decent response. "Let's just say Jack's cold was easier on him than me."

Her eyes narrow. "Serves you right."

I lean forward to get up. If she's not going to leave, I have to before her attitude drains me of all my remaining energy.

"Wait. Don't go." She mutters something.

I pause, but have no intention of getting cozy.

"Listen," she says, attention on the grass. "I'm sorry you're so sick."

I lift my eyebrows. Since when has Vivian been sorry for anything? She takes off her beanie and flattens her wild hair. I glance at her longboard lying on its side by my mailbox.

Her gaze follows mine. "Oh, and sorry about that."

I never thought I'd hear an apology out of her mouth, let alone two. "No harm," I say.

I tap my right foot, then my left. The neighbor's dog lets out a stream of barks. Maybe I should go inside. It's hard enough for one of us to have a normal conversation with anyone else. Trying to have one together is basically impossible. But she's still standing there, looking at my house, my lawn, my mailbox.

"Do you live around here?" I ask.

"Yeah. Just on the other side of the park."

I nod. That's good. Maybe I should invite her to go back home. I check my phone but there's still no response from Kyler. It's almost dinnertime, though. That would be a good excuse to go back inside. My stomach growls, giving me the perfect cue. "I should probably get going."

"Oh. Right."

I stand up and turn toward the door. I'm already turning the knob when Vivian says, "Hey, Kate."

I glance over my shoulder.

She crosses the grass and stops at the base of my front porch. "I'm sorry for giving you such a hard time."

I release the round knob and let my hand fall. A head of curly hair catches my attention and my heart trips a beat. But it's just a woman across the street, throwing luggage into

159

the trunk of a two door sports car. Vivian shifts and I focus my eyes on her.

I still haven't figured out how to respond. Do I tell her it's okay? That I'm over it? No, that would just give her permission to keep picking on new kids. But if I tell her it's not okay, she might start a fight—one that I wouldn't be able to win right now. And then she'd continue her old habits anyway. Especially since this attempt at making friends isn't going so well. There's no good option.

"I didn't know you rode a longboard," I finally say. Why not change the subject?

A faint smile lifts her face. "Yeah. Charlie comes along sometimes."

"And Jack?"

She frowns.

Apparently not. "That's great that Charlie rides. He's a fun kid." And he now sounds like a baby goat. I want to be nice to Vivian, but I can't think of anything else to talk about. My phone vibrates and I read the new text.

I'm almost home with dinner.

As much as I want it to be from Kyler, this isn't really his home. And that's not his number. A long, quiet minute later, Mom pulls into the driveway and parks the car. I can smell the cheese pizza before she takes out the square box. Vivian strolls back to her board, picks it up, and hovers near the edge of my yard.

After Mom shuts the car door with her hip, she says, "I got more nebulizer meds."

I clear my throat and she pauses—only then does she notice Vivian.

"Oh. I didn't know you had a friend over, Kate."

160

My face burns. Friend is definitely a loose term. And I didn't invite her over. "Mom, this is Vivian. She just stopped by."

Mom's so excited, you'd think she just won a million dollars. She sets her things on the cement and hands me the pizza. "Maybe Vivian would like to stay for dinner," she says.

"No," Vivian and I respond in unison. We pause and look at each other. I go for a fake grin, but her eyebrows pinch together and her jaw twitches.

Her voice comes out edgy. "I have to get going. It was nice to meet you. See you later, Kate." She sets her board on the ground and zooms off, the wheels clicking over each crack in the sidewalk.

Maybe I don't miss school as much as I thought. Of course I have to be the bad girl now. There's probably no hope for either one of us to have a lot of friends. She has hers and I have mine. Simple. We should keep it that way.

"That wasn't very nice, Kate," Mom says. She opens the front door and I follow her in.

"Trust me, Mom. It was the nicest conversation I've had with her."

My phone buzzes and I balance the pizza in one arm to check the message.

I have to go grocery shopping with my dad tonight. You know how that goes. He still has a hard time. Reminds him too much of Mom. I might not make it over until tomorrow. Feel better and get some rest.

At least I have memories of eating pizza with Kyler. It makes it easier to think about him throughout the meal. And all through my therapy. I stare at the pictures on my walls and let his voice fill my head.

161

I look forward to tomorrow. It's the first time I'll hang out with him as the real me, outside of the hospital, without tubes and doctors and endless reruns of my karate lessons. It's nice to dream about Kyler in my fake world, but I can't wait to have him with me here. No more secrets and no more emotional walls.

I fall asleep that night with a faint cough and leftover aches from the hospital. Even those can't stifle my hope of another tomorrow.

Chapter 22

I'm almost done with my nebulizer treatments when Mom walks into my room the next evening. "Kyler's here."

I suck in the meds and pull the tube away from my mouth. "Can you entertain him for a few minutes?"

She tilts her head.

"Show him some karate skills, Mom. He'd love it."

She shrugs and shuts the door.

Once I finish my treatments, I head down the stairs. Normally, I could get there in less than a minute. It takes me at least five. Kyler's standing in the middle of the living room with his feet shoulder-length apart and both hands flexed. I wait to see what will happen.

Mom lifts his right arm. "Keep it stiff. You have to be ready at all times."

She mirrors him and they circle. I'm not sure whether they'd really fight, but I need to save Kyler before either one of us finds out.

"I said teach him, Mom. Not kill him."

Kyler keeps his eyes on Mom. "I've got this, Kate."

Mom swings her leg out and Kyler tries to jump over. His foot catches on her shoe and he falls back, barely missing

163

the end table on his way down. I shuffle toward him, but Mom offers a hand and helps him up before I get there. Not that he needs the help. His laugh fills the room and I sink into the couch beside him.

"Better luck next time," Mom says. She winks at us and makes her way to the kitchen. "You guys want any food?"

Kyler puts his arm around me and I tilt my head to see his face. "You hungry?"

"Only if you are."

That's never a question. "Sure, Mom," I call.

Kyler's finger trails down my arm and I nestle into his side. "How were things at the grocery store?" I ask him.

His chest shakes with a laugh. "My dad's funny. No matter how many times we go, he likes to pretend he doesn't know what he's doing."

I faintly recall him having trouble picking out chicken when I ran into them.

"Last night it was the milk. We had a twenty minute conversation about which kind of milk we should be drinking."

"And what did you decide?"

"We didn't. I grabbed the one closest to me and went to find the yogurt."

Kyler's fingers weave through mine. I inhale the clean scent of his aftershave. His heart pulses through his ribs, beating lightly against my ear.

"How are you feeling today," he asks.

There's still a dull pain in my back, but it's not enough to bother me. Not that anything would bother me after what I just went through in the hospital. "As good as can be expected."

"You sure?" He lifts my chin, his fingers cradling my jaw.

I consider telling him about my exhaustion but I'm staring at his eyes, his freckles—especially the one on his lip. Kyler's breath touches my face and I lean into him. The thumping in my chest makes it hard to breathe, hard to think. I focus on his gaze and watch it settle on my lips. His mouth pulls up on one side and his arm tightens around me, pulling me closer. I squeeze his fingers, letting my eyes shut while holding my breath.

And the doorbell rings.

My eyes fly open and Kyler leans back. Mom comes in but stops when she notices us. Her face turns a shade darker and she points to the door. "Is someone here?"

Kyler releases his hold on me and Mom opens the door.

Giana rushes in. "You're home," she says, handing me a bouquet of flowers. "I just knew you wouldn't die."

I lift an eyebrow. "Thanks for the vote of confidence. And also for the flowers." Too bad she couldn't wait another five minutes. Even one would've been better. We were seconds from kissing. My face is still warm and I'm all too aware of Giana's steady gaze. She looks at Kyler, then at me, and then she grins.

Another voice catches my attention. I didn't notice Mo over my handful of roses. The sweet scent blows toward me as he closes the front door.

Mom props her fists on her hips. "More food?" she asks.

I nod and she disappears. But not without an extra bounce to her step. She's seen all my friends in one day—even

165

my non-friend. This is definitely more than she could've asked for.

Mo puts a hand on Giana's shoulder. "Hey, Kate. It's good to see you again."

"You too." I cough. The room goes quiet. Everyone's eyes are on me, waiting for me to break apart. I'm a rundown cathedral with only a few walls holding me together. "I'm fine," I say, and Giana lets out a loud sigh.

Mo takes a seat. "So, what are we going to do?"

I have an idea. But it's not a group activity. Maybe if we choose something that doesn't take a lot of time, Giana and Mo will leave. Or maybe something boring would chase them away. As much as I like having them here, things were going pretty good before they came.

"Anyone bring a banjo?" I ask.

"Nope," Mo says.

Giana pretends to hold something in her arms. "Is that like a circular guitar?" She strums her imaginary instrument.

Kyler tries to hide his smile.

"How about a game?" Giana asks.

My body grows heavy just thinking about it. I won't be able to last long, no matter what we do.

Kyler grips my hand. "Spin the bottle?"

"I heard that," Mom says from the kitchen.

Yeah, there's not going to be any kissing with her around.

"What's going on at school?" I ask.

"Let's please talk about something else," Giana says.

Mo plays with her hair. "Don't mind her. She just doesn't want to tell you the news."

I sit up a little straighter. "I could do with some good

166

news." At least, I hope it's good.

"She's going to be prom queen."

Giana rolls her eyes. "I doubt that."

"But you're definitely in the royalty?" I ask. That's hard for anyone to accomplish, especially a new girl. Somehow, it doesn't surprise me though.

She's blushing now. "I was nominated by the National Honor Society."

"Really?" I ask.

Mo leans forward. "Giana helped—"

She slaps her hand over his mouth. "It doesn't matter what I did. I don't even know if I'm going to the dance."

Mo moves her hand. "I'm taking you."

"What?" Her eyes grow. "You're asking me now?"

Their voices lower to work out details and Kyler leans into me. "Do you want to go with me?" he whispers.

My insides flip and I hold onto the feeling. I don't need his question to be a big affair. Anything said with his voice, coming out of his lips, is enough for me. As much as I'd love to go to Prom, I have to be realistic. "I don't even know if I'll be able to go."

"Then we'll dance here."

In my living room? The smell of popcorn makes my stomach growl and a *ding* echoes from the kitchen. "It's awful quiet in there," Mom says. "I'm bringing the food in now."

I laugh. Prom with my mom as the only chaperone would be lots of fun.

Kyler untangles his arms from mine and jumps up. How does he have so much energy? I can barely think about getting off the couch, let alone racing across the room. He meets Mom outside the kitchen and helps her bring in drinks,

167

popcorn, and a bag of potato chips.

"I have dip too," she says on her way back to the kitchen.

She returns with a container in one hand. Kyler sets it on the table as Mom drops a handful of pills into my outstretched palm. It's funny how I just knew she'd bring them. It's so automatic, engrained in our routines. No one watches me slip them into my mouth and chase them down with a drink. It's not that they don't care. It's that they do. They give me my space and they let me be me.

I place a handful of popcorn on my plate and put one in my mouth. "You'll totally be queen," I tell Giana.

"Let's not start that again." She shoots me a look and bites into a chip. A second later, she says, "It should've been you, Kate."

I snort out a weak laugh. "You have to be in a club or on a team to get nominated, don't you? My club is one member only."

"Oh yeah, what's that?" she asks.

"The hospital club. And I don't think members can nominate themselves."

"Who needs to be nominated?" Kyler says. "Being the only member in a club makes you a queen already, right?"

Or a loner.

Giana waves her hand and we wait for her to finish her bite. "Let's have our own Prom. It's overrated anyway."

Mo gives her a sidelong look and I can tell Giana doesn't believe the words coming out of her mouth. She wouldn't have been so excited that Mo was asking her to the real thing. Not only does she want to go, she would probably love to be queen. And she'd make a good one, looking out for us peasants, spreading happiness around her.

"I'll vote for you," I tell her. "That is, if I'm there."

Giana grins. "You'll be there. You're looking better every second."

Looks are deceiving. Or Giana's good at lying.

My eyes grow heavy and the ache in my back tightens with each bite. I sink into the couch and decide to rest, just for a moment.

I close my eyes and picture prom in Paris. That's what the theme should be. Kyler can wear a tux and I'll buy a floor-length gown with a teardrop tiara for my head. We'll dance beneath the Eiffel Tower, swaying to the sound of his voice. He'll hold me close with twinkle lights sparkling through the darkness. We'll waltz along the cobblestones, our feet shuffling over the firm foundation.

And it's exactly how I feel. Firm. Safe. My mind sways back and forth, back and forth, back and...

Chapter 23

I wake up and my firm foundation is falling apart. My chest burns, rages with a fire that can't escape. My world's crumbling in a stream of pain. I'm falling, letting go of memories in order to focus on each breath. They don't come. I claw at the bed and yell for Mom.

How did I get in bed? When did I fall asleep? Why isn't she here yet?

Mom rushes in with a phone. I hear three beeps as she dials nine-one-one. My vision blurs and I can barely see through the black spots. Mom holds me until the ambulance arrives. The paramedics strap me to a bed and we race to the hospital. They're talking to me but I can't understand what they're saying. It's muffled and loud. It's just noise.

Noise and pain.

A cough tears through the pain and comes out as red blood.

Someone wipes my mouth and holds me down to strap an oxygen mask over my face.

I try to breathe in again. One shallow breath, but it's not enough. I can't get it to fill my lungs.

I can't focus, I can't breathe. I can't live like this.

I try to scream and everything starts slipping away.

The ambulance stops and they wheel me inside. I focus on the nurse, the tinted windows, the speckled ceiling. They mush together in one black blob that suffocates me.

I'm jostled to the side as my bed moves.

Or maybe I'm just moving…following the light and letting go of reality.

Mom, Giana, Kyler. They're all gone.

I tried to stay, but I can't hold on any longer.

* * *

My chest feels heavy and my arms are like dead weights. I can't move, can't think. I wonder if I'm dead or alive. This can't be heaven. Heaven wouldn't smell like bleach and soap. No, I'm alive.

I struggle to open my eyelids and glance around. My body is puffed up like a marshmallow and there are tubes in my hands, arms, nose, chest, and stomach. I think I'd rather be dead. I close my eyes and try to slip away again. I was gone…and I think I was okay with it. But now I'm alive. What if I have to go through that again? I breathe in and back out. My breaths are still shallow and the oxygen tube is bothering my ear.

What happened to me? I was enjoying a night with my friends and now I'm here. I must've fallen asleep.

I hear footsteps and Doc Perry's voice says, "I see you're awake."

Opening my eyelids, I find him standing next to me. "What happened?" My voice is soft and scratchy and it hurts to talk.

"Your lung collapsed again."

Of course it did. There's a tube coming out of my chest, tying me to the wall once again. Not only am I stuck in a prison, I'm shackled in place too.

Doc continues. "It's at a ten percent function level."

What? Ten percent? The number flashes through my brain like the time left on something almost done in the microwave. *I'm* almost done.

"And we found a new infection."

My stomach knots up and panic rises in my throat. Tears sting my eyes and I refuse to let them fall.

"Kate. This is serious."

Does it look like I'm laughing? If it didn't hurt so bad to talk, he'd get a load of my mind.

"We're doing all we can, but we might have to look at other options."

We both know there's only one other option.

"Luckily we are a certified lung transplant center. Your information is being processed and will soon be ready for evaluation."

I'm not surprised. We knew this was a possibility, but it's always been the last option.

Doc swallows. "Usually this process takes a considerable amount of time. Unfortunately, I don't think we have that."

In a nutshell…I'm as good as dead if things don't work out. My mind wants to shut down, but I know I need to hear more. I clear my thoughts and put on a straight face. Just like Mom. She sits on the couch, her eyes glazed and her hand crushing a tissue. I need her to tell me to stay, to tell me I'm her favorite girl, and tell me that there's still a best case scenario.

172

"We need to run a few more tests. I know how you must feel—"

Yeah right.

"But you can't be an active candidate for a transplant without a proper evaluation."

And that's when it begins. Doc wheels me down for more x-rays, blood tests, and an exercise test that I fail right away. I'm able to keep my emotions in check and treat myself as a lab rat. Do this, do that, don't think about it too much or I might just drift away. Mom stays by my side; her face is a reflection of my emotions. Shut off and in survival mode. We're visited by multiple physicians and specialists then interviewed by social workers and a psychiatrist. Mom does most of the talking and I continue to keep a straight face.

With all the interviews, tests, and regular therapy, I feel like a test patient. And each day I come closer to death. They won't let my friends visit me yet, and even mom has to dress down in surgical coverings. If I qualify for a transplant, we still have to wait for a match to come in. That can take as long as a few years. And like Doc Perry already said, I don't have three years. I don't even have three months. I'll be lucky to stay alive for three weeks.

Days later, the transplant surgeon finally shows up. He was out of town for another surgery and should be here in my room any moment. Mom's pacing back and forth between the door and the window that looks over a cement courtyard. There are bags under her eyes and her hair gets more frazzled each time she runs a hand through it.

"Mom, if you don't stop, you're going to be bald before he gets here."

173

She turns to me. I've never seen her look so worried. "I know. But...I just *can't* sit still. You don't understand."

I cringe. She doesn't think I'm worried too? Or maybe she doesn't think I understand how serious this is. I've thought about it every single day of my life. Of course I would understand. Besides, it's not her dying...it's me. But maybe she's worried about something else. I shouldn't think the worst of Mom when she's always been the best.

Maybe she's worried about paying for all this. That has to be it. Why didn't I think of it before? There's no way my mom can afford a transplant. I don't know exactly how much it costs, but it has to be thousands, if not millions. There's no way I can stop her, though. That's like agreeing to my sudden death and her lonely life. Neither one of us want that. I close my mouth and let her pace. Her shoes click across the linoleum and I drum my fingers in a sporadic rhythm.

Soon there's a knock at the door. Mom flinches and turns with her hands clasped. Even then, they shake worse than a tree in a windstorm. Her worry makes me want to be calmer. If she can't hold it together, one of us has to do it.

The door opens and Doc Perry comes in first, followed by a tall man with sandy-colored hair and pale skin. The man freezes right inside the door and his eyes flick back and forth between Mom and me. Only then do I realize how familiar he looks. Those eyes, the edge to his jaw, the way his hair falls across his forehead, just like it did sixteen years ago.

The silence is thick with tension and even Doc Perry notices something weird. "Do you know each other?"

Know? How about knew? I clench my fists tight and think of a million karate moves. Mom gave me permission to use them if Dad ever showed up, and here he is. But I don't really feel like hitting him—the action's just been engraved in my brain. Even though I know he tried to come back once, I never really thought I'd ever see him again. Especially here, like this. He's a transplant surgeon? Apparently his fear of reality wasn't enough to stop him in the medical field.

"Mom?" I say through clenched teeth, my eyes focused on her pale face. "Did you know?"

She nods once, small and short. *This* is why she was so nervous. Not because of the money and not because of the risk—it was because she knew Dad was a transplant surgeon and that he might be the one coming. Why didn't she tell me? Now I'm mad at both of my parents. I grab a dart and roll it between my fingers with my eyes shut tight. I'm like a time bomb waiting to blow. If I look too hard at everything around me, the fuse will ignite and I'll burst into a million pieces.

Don't light. Don't burst. Don't throw the dart.

"I've reviewed your case," Dad says. His voice is deep and serious. "It seems that you're in great need of a transplant or your lungs will fail you completely."

"Wait." My eyes fly open, my breaths quick. The sadness in Dad's expression ignites the fuse and I nearly explode. "You reviewed my case? That's all you're going to say? No 'Hi there? How are you?' Is no one else freaking out that my dad's my transplant doc? Is that even legal?" I clench my jaw.

Doc Perry goes rigid and he looks between the three of us. "It can't be." He turns to Mom. "You didn't say anything."

Dad raises a hand. "That's not important right now—"

"Not important?" I ask, my tone rising with each syllable.

175

"No," he says. "We'll talk about that later. Trust me, I'm *very* interested to hear the details. But right now we need to get things going for your transplant. Getting you on the list is one thing, finding a match is going to be the tricky part. Your size is going to be a big factor. I can tell you right now there aren't many people on the transplant list that are as petite as you. That *can* be a really good thing."

Oh good. I was hoping there was a bright side to all this doom.

"The problem is that most donors are either smaller children or taller adults. We don't see a lot of donors who would qualify to give you their lungs."

A sliver of dread works its way through my heart. He just sealed my fate. Will things ever go right for me?

Dad folds his arms. "We're going to have a final meeting with the transplant team here and I'll let you know when your status goes active."

Doc Perry picks up my large file and opens the door. "Kate's right about one thing. You can't do surgery on your own family member."

I stay quiet. Doc Perry has my back on this one.

Dad nods. "I'll call Dr. Farrow today. He should be able to fill in. Until he gets here, I'm the only one who can lead this team. And if worse comes to worst, I'm going to do the surgery if I'm the only one here. Besides, I didn't even know I *had* family." Dad steps closer to Mom and me. "The first break I get, I'm coming back. We have some catching up to do and there are things I'll explain, but I need some answers too."

He turns quickly and exits the room. The door clicks shut and I face Mom with a million questions battling to escape the tip of my tongue. Finally, one gets free. "Why didn't you tell me?"

Mom's head drops and she rubs her temples. "I just found out a couple of years ago. I didn't know how to tell you. Besides, I had hoped it wouldn't come to this point. At least, not this soon."

"But you could've said *something* before he walked in the room."

She shakes her head. "I wasn't sure if it was going to be him, Kate. Besides, it wouldn't have done any good. You have enough to worry about already."

"Oh, I see." Not really. She lied to me. She could have told me about it a year ago when I was doing okay. At least then I would have known the reunion might happen at some point. And here we are, shoved together with Dad in a situation that could take months, if not longer, to resolve. I want to be happy that he knows I'm alive but I don't even know what he's thinking or feeling. Ticked, I bet.

I know nothing about him and he knows nothing about me. We were dead to each other and now we're both alive—at least for a little while. And now I'm dependent on him to help me survive. I'm his patient and he's here to treat me as a surgeon. Yes, he wants an explanation, but that doesn't mean he wants a daughter. Especially one who's about to die.

If he ran before, he might run again when this is all over. And if he doesn't, there's a chance I will. As it stands, I might die before he has the opportunity to leave.

"How's my favorite girl?" Mom asks in a soft voice.

I close my eyes and breathe in. As mad as I am about the whole thing, I can't blame it all on Mom. She's always thinking of me and I know this isn't an exception. But that

177

doesn't settle the anger bubbling inside me. Everything from the past few days has built up—meeting Dad was just the final blow.

"I'm fine, Mom. I just need some time to digest everything."

She pats my leg and I hear her retreat to the couch. I try to think of Dad but there are too many loose ends that don't connect. My mind wanders, searching for something safe to focus on. Not Mom and not anything to do with my disease. Within seconds, I've found the perfect thing, but it takes all my remaining energy to push away the distractions and find Kyler's face. I hold on tight to the image and listen to his voice. It clears my head of the mess I call my life.

I'm always preparing for the worst and now that it's here, I'm scrambling for hope. Hope is everywhere; I just have to find it. If I die, there has to be something good about it. And that one good thing, that one hope that I cling to, is that the angels in heaven will sound like Kyler. If they do, somehow everything will be okay.

Chapter 24

As much as Mom doesn't want to leave me, she has to go to work the next morning. An hour later, there's a knock on the door. That's how the nurses, doctors, and everyone else announce their arrival. I'm used to it, and most of the time I don't even tell them to come in, they just do it because they need to be here anyway. What I'm not used to is having my long lost dad step around my curtain.

I still haven't decided what to say to him. I feel like I should love him, but I don't even know him. Smoothing the blanket over my legs, I say, "Is this a doctor's visit or a parent check-up?"

Dad comes farther into the room and folds his arms. "We need to talk."

I press my hands into my legs. "You didn't answer my question."

His arms fall. "I'm not here about your evaluation or anything. The board meets in a few hours but this is just about me and you...and I guess your mom." He clears his throat and rocks back on his heels. "Is she at work?"

"*Someone* has to pay for all this." I wave my hands around then let them collapse.

Dad rubs his face. "Look." He exhales slowly. "I don't really know what to say. I mean, I thought you were *dead*."

His voice catches and a knot forms in my stomach. I shrug and try to look anywhere but at the obvious exhaustion sagging below his eyes. It wouldn't do any good to point out that I might actually be dead soon if he can't help me. I go for a change of subject instead. "How long have you been a transplant surgeon?"

His face tightens into a more business-like, hardened expression. As much as I'd like to get to know him, it might be better to not involve feelings. Not yet. "Four years."

Okay? Not sure where I thought that question would take me. Obviously…nowhere. "Why did you decide to do lung transplants?"

Dad's shoulders fall and he sits on the edge of the couch. "For years I tried to run from anything related to cystic fibrosis. Eventually, I got tired of running. I started researching it and I couldn't get enough. It became an obsession. My life up to that point wasn't worth much and I needed a change. That's why I stopped by to see your mom. And that's when I found out you were gone."

The hollow look in his gaze nags at me, closes off my throat, and makes it hard to swallow.

"Did she even tell you I stopped by?" he asks.

Blank expression, blank expression. Just tell him facts. "I was sitting in the front room."

Dad cusses under his breath. "Of course you were. That shouldn't surprise me. Your mom's always been to the point and very open."

Except for when she found out about his new career. She kept that one to herself.

180

"But why didn't you say something?" he asks.

A heavy pressure makes its way up my throat. "I didn't know *what* to say."

He blinks. "Hi? Nice to see you?"

I clench my fist. "That would've been a lie. You left us. There's nothing nice about that."

Dad clears his throat and looks at the ground. I press my lips together and clasp my trembling hands. The silence seeps through me and pushes against the hard shell I've created.

When Dad lifts his face, his eyes are swimming in tears. He rubs at them and wipes his hand on his pants. "Instead of giving you someone to rely on after we got your first test results, I left. I was scared and I hoped it would help me forget. But it didn't. You were constantly on my mind. I knew if I came to visit, your mom wouldn't be happy about it, but I wasn't prepared for the news." He pauses. "My chance to make up the lost years was suddenly gone."

He thought he could make up eight years? That's eight birthdays, several lost teeth, and millions of treatments. Even more now.

Dad wipes his face again. "After I found out you were gone, I knew I had to do something with my life or I'd slip into a deep depression. My studies helped me focus and eventually I pulled through. I got my feet on the right track and I found something to live for…something that helped me feel like I was making things up to you."

I lift my eyebrows and clench my teeth, afraid to trust my own voice.

"I wasn't there for you," he says. "But now I'm a certified CF doctor and lung surgeon. I've performed multiple

181

transplants, and I find that helping others with CF has been my only connection to you. I hope it wasn't all for nothing…" His voice trails off and he takes a steadying breath. "I know it won't be easy, but I hope one day you'll give me a chance."

His eyes plead with me. It's the same look I've seen other dads share with their children, one that I've been jealous of my whole life. And now I'm getting it from a complete stranger. As much as I don't want it to, the wall holding back my resentment begins to crack. He's my flesh and blood and no matter what he's done before, he's a good person now. Maybe, one day, I can grow to love him.

As long as I have enough time.

There's another knock on the door and Ember comes in with my pre-lunch meds. Halfway into the room, she stops. "Oh, sorry. I didn't know your doctor was here. I can come back in a few minutes if you'd like."

Apparently she hasn't heard the news. I wave her in. "He's just visiting."

Her eyebrows shoot up. "Oh…okay."

I exhale loudly and my stomach growls. "He's my dad. Now please give me my pills, I'm hungry."

Dad stands up and comes to my side. "I'm just heading out to meet with the board. I'll be back with the results soon. Keep your head up, Kate. I'm on your side now."

I stare at him and nod my head slightly. Something stirs inside me; it fills me with warmth and pricks my heart with a feeling I can't describe. Maybe it's the first step to accepting him as more than a medical expert.

He leaves the room and Ember sets my lunch in front of me without another word.

* * *

182

By late afternoon, the pain in my back seems worse and my whole body aches from being in the same position for so long. I need to walk, run—anything but sit in this bed. My eyes are still closed from taking a nap and I don't want to open them to reality. So I keep them shut and think about what I might be missing at school.

It seems like so long ago that I went to school. Even though I don't know a lot of students, I can picture a few people perfectly. The flirty look that consumes Vivian when she's around Jack, Max's puffed up chest when the teacher does anything to highlight the fact that he's much younger—and smarter—than everyone else, and Charlie's blonde hair bouncing as he ran from me that first day. I remember the last thing he said to me, about losing my attitude. I'd like to think my conversation with Vivian changed that, but I'm not sure it did anything.

The door to my room opens and I hear someone close to me say, "Shhh." It sounds like Mom's clipped shushing which means she must've come in while I was asleep.

"How is she?" It's Dad.

Great. Just what I need, Mom and Dad together. Whatever they have to say to each other, they can do it without my opinion. I'll just keep pretending I'm out of it.

Mom never answers Dad's question, at least not out loud.

Eventually, he asks, "Why did you lie to me?"

"Are we really going to do this here?" Mom snaps.

"Yes." His voice is heavy. "I've tried to contact you multiple times since that day and not once have you answered my calls."

"You made your decision."

183

I cringe at her tone. Dad's got a lot of nerve confronting her, especially now. She's going to be a lot harder to crack than I am.

"I've changed. Can't you see? I've made something of my life. Stop trying to push me away."

His words sting like a fresh wound. They remind me too much of Charlie's plea and something clicks in my brain. Now I know why I push people away. I thought it was just because of my disease but maybe it's more than that. Maybe I'm so good at it because I live with the expert.

"What?" Mom asks, her voice getting louder. "You're telling me that you suddenly care about being a part of my life just because Kate's still alive?"

"She's *our* daughter, not just yours."

There's a pause and I hold my breath.

"No. She *is* mine. That was your decision. And we're doing just fine without you."

Dad exhales a long sigh. "*Please*. All I ask is that you let me help."

"Help with what? You want to hold her hand? Go ahead and try. The only thing you can do here is what we're paying you to do."

Another pause and I count the seconds until someone talks again.

One.

Two.

Three.

What's going on? Why aren't they saying anything?

Four.

Five.

"Listen," Dad says.

184

My built up tension releases.

"There *is* one thing I can help with besides just doing my job."

"What's that?" Mom asks.

He waits a few beats. "Money."

This time the silence is good. It means Mom's considering the offer. But will she really take it? We both know she can't afford my transplant but with everything happening, we haven't had time to discuss the details.

"I can't take it," Mom whispers.

"I'm not asking you to." Dad's voice is stronger now, louder. "I'm giving it to you. I was never the dad I should've been. I have a good job with only myself to support. I know there's no way I can ever make up for the way I was, but maybe this will help you see who I am now. You don't have to love me...you don't even have to like me. I'm doing this for both of you, but you can tell yourself I'm doing it for Kate."

I clench my blankets and feel the delicate barricade around my heart turn to dust. I have a dad. Here, in my room. Someone who wants to take care of me even though he's never been around before. He's here now and he really wants to help. If I can't love him as a dad yet, I can at least appreciate what he's doing for us.

His footsteps thud against the floor, crossing the room. They stop and I breathe once before he says, "Kate. You're now active on the transplant list."

I open my eyes and look at him. "How did you know I was awake?"

His mouth lifts into a weak smile. "I'm a doctor. I can tell what a sleeping person looks like."

He probably knows what a dying person looks like too. *Me*. I shiver and he gazes at me for one short moment before he glances at Mom and leaves the room.

"Are you going to accept his offer?" I ask her, even though it was clear he wasn't giving her a choice. I need something to break the brittle ice around the whole "dad" topic.

Mom shrugs. "I just hope they can find you a match. I'll worry about how we're going to pay for it later."

Even if they don't find a match, my hospital bills are probably more than she can handle...for the rest of her life. And if I die, there's a funeral to pay for. Either way, I know Dad will offer to cover any expenses.

I think of another question and try to hold it back, but it has to be said. "Is it possible that he's really changed and wants another chance?"

Her whole body deflates. "I don't know, honey. There's no way around him, though, so we just have to hope that he's at least committed until things get better."

Get better or end completely. Now that I've seen Dad, it's going to be harder for Mom to convince me to push him away. Maybe she won't even try. If they don't find a match for my lungs, none of it will matter in the end.

Mom needs Dad as much as he needs her. I don't care if they never fall in love again, but with everything going on these last few weeks, I've discovered that people really do care, and they make life worth living. If I die, Mom's going to need someone. She's always telling me to find friends, but where are hers?

And where are mine right now? Hopefully they can come in soon. I need a distraction and I need their happiness.

Everything here is doom and gloom. Mom's no help now that she's got the thought of Dad weighing her down. Without Giana's optimism and Kyler's ability to soothe my worries, the hospital walls feel like they're closing in, ready to smash me—if my lungs don't kill me first.

I need people, and Mom needs them too.

We can't do this alone anymore.

Chapter 25

Dad comes in the next morning as doctor. He ups my pain meds to keep me stable and skips pleasantries to get to the details.

"I was right about the size of your lungs, Kate," he says. "There isn't an exact match on the whole waiting list. But there also hasn't been a donor with the same size and blood type for three years."

I nod, numbing my mind to the information. The new meds have made everything a bit fuzzy, but I can still figure out the difference between high and low chances of finding a match before it's too late. If I'm going to die, though, I want to live first.

"Can my friends visit yet?" I ask.

Dad stumbles on an answer and I wonder if he's trying to be Dad now or super strict medic. "They'll have to wear an isolation gown just like your mom and me."

Ah, that ought to be fun. "Is that a yes?"

"Do you have a lot of friends?"

As much as I'd like to sound popular, I shake my head. "I think there are only two who'd come."

"I'll tell Doctor Perry and your nurse that I've approved two visitors. What are their names?"

"Giana and Kyler."

He writes them down on a piece of paper. "They'll be put on a strict time limit, but I don't see why they can't come see you. It's probably for the best."

It *is* for the best. There's only so much a bundle of useless darts and old architecture magazines can do for me. And having a conversation isn't one of them.

"Thanks...Dad." The word jumbles around my mouth like a foreign piece of food. Instead of rolling off my tongue, it gets caught in the middle and my brain screams at me to never say it again.

Dad seems hesitant to respond, like he couldn't believe I actually used the word. "You're welcome. I'll go talk to your nurse right now and we'll get you set up."

Okay, so it might be a good thing to have my dad involved—not only as a doctor but as a father who wants to make up for years of neglect. I can almost hear Giana's laugh...but it isn't as exciting as the thought of Kyler's caressing voice.

* * *

Word must travel quickly because Giana shows up that afternoon. I hardly recognize her through the blue isolation gown hiding her whole body. There's a mask covering her mouth and a net around her hair. Mom doesn't even dress down that much. The whole thing makes me laugh and instantly, I feel like I can breathe a little better.

"Don't I look fabulous?" Giana asks.

"Yeah, like a bloated blueberry."

Her eyebrows dance. "Did you just call me fat?"

189

The question makes me laugh harder and I'm gasping for a decent breath. Of course it turns into a cough and I have to wait for everything to settle down before we can carry on our conversation.

"No more jokes," I say. "You have to be all serious and tell me the boring things that are happening at school."

Giana nods her head like a soldier and sits down. "Boring is right. A new kid came in and Vivian didn't do a thing."

I blink. "What? Really?"

"It may have something to do with her new boyfriend."

My jaw drops. "She finally hooked up with Jack?"

"Nope. Seems like Charlie's had the hots for her for some time."

I nearly choke on that piece of news. "Isn't he younger than her?"

"And shorter. It's the weirdest thing I've ever seen."

And it would explain why he felt the need to point out the details of his friendship with her before they officially got together. Maybe he won't care so much that I have an attitude anymore. As long as he has his blue-haired girlfriend, he should be good. I won't judge him for it, but I need to get the image of them out of my head.

"Quick," I say. "Tell me something else before I lose my lunch."

Giana laughs. "Well, I have a new idea for cystic fibrosis awareness." The way she wrings her hands and waits for my reply makes me think I'm not going to like it.

"And…that's…"

"I don't want to tell you everything," she says, rushing through her words. "But I need your permission to let others know you have it."

A knot forms in my throat and I have a hard time breathing past it. "Really?"

She nods, her eyes serious and set in a way that I know she won't back down. Not when it comes to a good cause.

The lump in my throat sinks to my stomach and I think I'm going to be sick. I've kept my disease a secret for so long, I'm not sure I can give her permission even if I want to.

Do I want to? I think back to the few weeks I went to school here. Most likely, I'll only see a few of those students again. If I make it out of this hospital, school might already be out and graduation might be done with. I'll have to finish my studies at home and earn my diploma when I get the chance.

The only other person I care about already knows I have CF. But there's something else holding me back. Maybe it's the possibility that if I live, people might recognize me and then they'd know. They might treat me differently, like I'm contagious or fragile. If they see me, though, that will mean I actually survived. And living is definitely the better alternative to them finding out because I died. Before I can back down from my sudden decision, I look at Giana and say, "Okay."

"Thank you, Kate. You won't regret it." She checks the clock on the wall. "I have to go soon so I can finish planning and get everything started."

"Already? You can't tell me anything?"

"You'll find out soon enough."

I try to think of something to keep Giana here. Our time's not up yet and I can't be left alone. "My dad's here."

Giana freezes. "What?"

I tell her about the unhappy reunion.

"Whoa," she says. "Are you okay with it?"

I shrug. "Until the other doc shows up, I have to be."

"But now he knows you're alive. That's a good thing, right?"

"I'm not sure. He could still leave."

Giana smiles. "He won't. You'll get your lungs and you can all be a happy family."

"Ha. Yeah right." I'm not sure we could ever have that. Or that I'd even want it.

"Things will get better."

I decide to change the subject instead of dwell on her optimism. "Speaking of things...how *are* things with prom royalty?"

Her cheeks glow pink beneath her mask. "Like I said, I've gotta run."

"Wait. That's not fair."

Her energy dies a little as she exhales. "I'm sorry I can't stay longer. I really do have a meeting to get to. But everything's good. They won't announce the winner until that night anyway. See you later." And she's gone, out the door, down the hall, and into the fresh air of the world I can only glimpse through a square pane of glass.

I sink into my pillow and try to relax. The pain meds still kind of mix my thoughts together, but they can't stop the adrenaline that Giana's visit gave me. It takes most of the evening to clear away the image of Vivian and Charlie together. Not to mention the thought of Giana hanging up posters that say, "Kate has CF. That's why she's not here and that's why you need to listen to me and help support this cause."

What did I agree to? I toss and turn all night, and by the time I finish physical therapy the next morning, I'm more than willing to take the sleep aid Ember offers. I wait for it to ease away my rambling thoughts and take me somewhere without dreams of school, CF awareness, or stubborn parents.

* * *

The sleep aid must've worked because when I open my eyes, my world is groggy. Ember hurries to give me my meds, make me eat, and start my therapy. I want to scream at her to slow down, but maybe it's just that my mind can't keep up. As much as I loved the rest, I'm not sure the sleeping pill was worth swimming through thick air to accomplish these everyday tasks.

"You have a visitor," Ember says after everything's finally done.

"Really? Who?" *Please-say-Kyler-please-say-Kyler.*

She winks. "You'll see."

My heart leaps and I almost jump out of bed to keep up with it. "How long has he been here?"

"A little while. He had to wait until we were finished. I'll go right now and prep him with his space suit." She pulls up my blankets and looks me in the eye. "I'm sorry, but you'll only have a few minutes with him. Your Dad is coming soon to give you the latest report on your recent x-rays and transplant status."

"Can't he wait?" Maybe I could play the daughter card on him to get more time with Kyler.

"I'll see what I can do," Ember says. "Either way, visitors can only stay fifteen minutes."

She grabs her things and disappears behind the curtain blocking the door. The same door that hides Kyler. Why isn't

193

he in here yet? My hands fidget and my legs ache to move. There's a pounding in my chest and a dance in my stomach. My whole body is alive with anticipation.

I don't even hear a knock before a blue-garbed body steps around the curtain. It's like a magic trick. *Poof.* Kyler's here. Although, I think the real trick will be getting my heart to slow down so the nurses don't race back in.

"Hey, Kate."

I grin and suppress the happy laugh bubbling up my throat. "Kyler. It's so good to see you."

He glances at the blue hospital get-up. "Can you even see me?"

I shrug. What matters is that I can *hear* him. His voice has the same effect it always has. It frees me from this place and makes the sun shine brighter than I've seen in days. "I'm sorry you have to wear that."

He blinks and I wonder what his mouth looks like. Is he smiling? Frowning? I can't tell what he's thinking.

"It's not a big deal." His eyes soften. "How are you?"

The question makes me want to laugh. And I do. It comes out as a helpless, defeated sort of chortle. "You want the truth?"

He steps closer and nods.

It's suddenly hard to talk. Usually I just tell people I'm fine…but I'm *not* fine. And it isn't until now that I've even considered how I really feel. I cover my face with my hands and fall to pieces, sniffing and coughing, in a pool of tears.

Kyler pulls at my hands with his gloved fingers and I hold onto him with everything left in me. "Shh," he says. "Please don't cry, Kate." His voice catches.

"I'm so scared," I whisper. I'm afraid if I say it any louder, everyone will hear and then they'll know.

"It's okay to be scared," he says, stroking my hair with his other hand and wiping away a few tears. "Just hold on. You'll get through this."

I sniff loudly. "How?"

"Well, Giana's doing a fundraiser for you. She's trying to earn money for your transplant."

I blink away more tears. "She is?"

That must be her big plan. Not to spread the word just for her niece, but to help find a cure for me. Even if it's just money for a set of lungs, it's the best cure for now.

Kyler must see the hope in my eyes. "She already printed flyers, posters, and has links on the internet for a big fundraiser raffle event this weekend. There are companies who've donated and others who are matching donation percentages."

Whoa. He's using big words and my slow brain is losing track of everything. But I know this is all happening because of Giana. One person really *can* make a difference. But it won't matter in the end if the right lung match doesn't come in time. How horrible is it that I'm waiting for someone else to die so I can live? Fresh tears trail down my cheek and Kyler catches them as they slip off my chin.

"Giana said she'll come visit you Saturday night after everything's over," Kyler tells me. "She won't have time to come back before then."

I'm not sure what I'll say to her. What can I say to someone who's done so much for me? More tears, more sniffles. "Kyler."

He leans closer and squeezes my hand.

It kills me to say the next words. "You realize I might not ever leave this hospital."

"Let's not think about that. Let's talk about what we're going to do when you get better." He pauses. "We could find another gallery."

I smile with the thought of having him so close to me again. I shut my eyes and imagine his arms around me. "What else?"

He twirls a strand of my hair around his finger and my heart skips.

"I've been learning some French music," he whispers. "Maybe I could teach you to sing with me."

I give a helpless laugh and open my eyes.

Kyler's gaze pierces through me and pulls at different chords in my heart. I never imagined eyes could sing, but his move with a melody of their own. They sparkle through the tears on my lashes and drop down to glance at my lips. The melody becomes a symphony, making his eyes light up with fire as they meet mine again.

He pulls his hand away from my hair and tugs at the mask covering his mouth until his lips are showing. My heart thumps up my throat and steals any words that might escape. I know he's not supposed to breathe on me, but I don't want to die without making this moment worth every last breath.

Kyler's face inches closer to mine and I shut my eyes. "Kate."

No! Don't talk, just go before I change my mind.

It seems like forever before he says anything. "Do I have to sign a contract?"

I reach around his neck and pull his lips to mine. The second they touch, my insides collapse and I melt into him.

196

The kiss is soft and warm and I can't seem to get enough air…but I don't want to stop.

Kyler pulls back and I gasp. He lifts the mask over his mouth and says, "Sorry."

I stare at him, wanting more, wishing he wouldn't apologize for making me feel so alive. "Please, don't say that."

"But you might get sick."

I lift my hands in defeat. "I can't get much worse. And it was worth it."

Kyler's eyes light up. "Should we try it again?"

Yes? Okay, maybe not. Not yet. I don't want to forget the first one. "Can you sing me a song instead?"

He holds my hand and sings a thousand kisses to my heart until Dad comes and Ember chases Kyler away.

Chapter 26

Dad steps away from the x-ray screen and turns toward me with concern etched on every part of his face. I swallow and wait for the bad news. Even Kyler's lingering kiss can't erase the instant dread in my gut.

"I'm afraid to tell you that your lungs aren't healing well from this last collapse. We're only up to fifteen percent function and it should be higher by now."

I clench my hands and let the words slip through my brain. The information can't settle. If it does, I won't be able to hold myself together much longer. I swallow again and try to breathe evenly.

"Now what?" I ask. "Any news on a donor?"

Dad shakes his head and his worry lines deepen. "Nothing new there either."

What he really means is there's nothing good to tell me. I hold onto the last strings of hope and tighten them into a knot. I won't give up and I won't give in. Not yet. There's still air left in my crippled lungs.

"I have some meetings to attend," Dad says. "But I'll check back with you later."

I keep a blank expression as he walks out of the room—the room with four walls, one window, and countless medical supplies keeping one girl alive. But for how much longer?

I need Kyler right now but instead, I get a message from Ember that he won't be able to visit again until after the fundraiser. That should make me happy, excited that he wants to be a part of something that will benefit my future. But my future isn't looking too bright. It's dark, lonely, and filled with the smell of sterilized metal. I can almost feel my body breaking down. Time drags as I memorize the tan canvas of my walls. Eventually, the images in my head swirl together in a mix of doubt and fear and I drift into a thoughtless stupor.

Mom comes in Saturday morning and sets a tray of food in front of me. "I told Ember I'd give you your breakfast."

She hands me my pills and I take them.

"Better eat up. It smells delicious."

I keep my hands in my lap.

"The fundraiser is today," she says. Her chipper voice gets more forced every time she talks.

I nod.

Mom walks past me and sits on the bed. "Sounds like there's going to be a big turnout."

I blink twice.

"Kate." She grabs my hand and waits for me to look her in the eyes. It takes me almost a minute to finally give in. The moment I do, I wish I hadn't. Tears stream down her face and she squeezes her eyes shut as she wipes her nose with a tissue. Her grip tightens around my hand like she thinks I'll slip away.

It's definitely a possibility.

I try to wrap my fingers around hers, but my grip is weak. I'm still drowning in the bad news. I stare at Mom and try to feel something...anything. I love her, I'll miss her, but it's like my body has shut down my ability to connect with others.

"I'm sorry, Mom." It's all I can say because even if I can't feel it, I know it should be said.

"I'm sorry too." Her voice shakes. "It's so hard to see my favorite girl like this."

She doesn't even ask how her favorite girl is doing. It's the first time I haven't heard her say the words as she walks into my room. She probably doesn't want to know more than she can see.

Mom sniffles. "I hate to leave you, but I can't stay long. Giana asked me to come down for the fundraiser so everyone could see who they'll be benefitting."

I nod once. It sounds like a good idea. "It's okay. I'll be here when you get back."

Hopefully. I'm not sure I'm even here right now. My brain's stuck in limbo, numb to everything around me. I should care that she won't stay with me on her day off. But I can't.

She walks out the door and I sink into my bed. My gaze switches from the wall to the speckled ceiling. Images float through my mind: an old building, a song in a different language, a lock of curly hair, a single freckle. Those things should mean something. I know the name of the building. It's the Pantheon Paris, but the image doesn't affect me like it should. It's like I've lost my desire to visit France. Maybe because I know I never will.

And the freckle? It's Kyler's, but for some reason, his name doesn't ignite the fire that usually burns within me. I'm like an empty hearth, freshly cleaned and really cold. The images drift away and I'm left with the only thing that's real: the dark specks that are scattered across the ceiling.

I start to count them and lose track. It's like counting the stars or counting freckles.

Freckles.

What's wrong with me? Why can't I focus?

A knock at the door startles me.

"Kate?"

My dad walks in with a stethoscope in one hand and a strange package in the other. He sets the package on a side table and approaches me with the medical device. Doctor. He's my doctor and he's here to check my stats.

Dead. Dead. Dead.

I can't get the word out of my mind. One day he'll come in to check me and there won't be anything left to check. The cool metal touches the skin on my chest and I inhale slowly. Dad's saying something but it sounds like medical words. Mumble jumble.

I don't care.

I *can't* care.

I won't care.

It's all over.

"Kate!"

I lift my gaze and look at him. "Why are you yelling at me?"

"Did you hear a word I said?"

His face is so stern. Why is he acting like that?

His mouth pulls into a frown. "Please. Stay with me."

201

I point to the tubes tying me to the wall. "I don't think I have a choice."

"No. You don't have a choice but I won't let you go."

I shrug.

He crosses the room and comes back to set the package on my lap. "Open this."

"What is it?"

He reaches down and pulls at the brown paper. Once it's off, I'm staring at a carving of The Gallery of Kings. I count the men standing in robes. Twenty-eight. A woodsy smell fills my nose and I touch the edge of a crown.

Something stirs inside me. I let it spark and pulse as I press my fingertip into a blank expression on one of the faces. It's just like me. Blank. I dig deep in my brain to make a connection. Notre Dame, French architecture, mini statue, date with Kyler.

Kyler! Kisses, freckles, friends, life. The memories slam into place and I gasp...then cough.

Dad rubs my back. "Breathe, Kate. Breathe."

The coughing continues and I wonder what just happened. It's like my thoughts were locked away, protected in a secret place even I couldn't reach. "What was that?"

Dad helps me lie back and sits on the chair beside me. "A mild dissociative episode. It's normal for someone under so much stress."

I try to think back through the haze. "Mild? I thought I was losing it." My hands are still on the statue so I lift it up to memorize the tiny details in each staff. "I've seen this before. Where did you get it?"

"It was at a local art show recently."

"Yes, I went there with Kyler." I freeze and look at Dad. "Did Kyler put you up to this?"

He tilts his head side to side. "Is that his name?"

I lift an eyebrow.

Dad holds up a hand. "Okay, okay. I might've talked to your friends. But I wanted to give you something and they helped me out since I don't know much about you...*yet*."

"You're trying to buy your way into my life?"

He gives a shaky laugh. "Please don't get upset, I'm doing my best. I hope to do more than pay for a statue."

"Me too," I whisper. Not because I want his money but because if he uses his money, it would be for a lung transplant. And that would mean I'd be around longer, which would also give me a chance to have a dad.

"I also brought you this." Dad holds out an ancient handheld video game.

"Does that even work?"

"Of course it does. Turn it on."

I do as he says and the first thing to pop up on the screen is a six-ringed bullseye. I give him a pointed look. "You really *did* do your homework."

He lifts an eyebrow. "What do you mean?"

I barely laugh. "Seriously?"

His eyes are wide. "Kyler didn't tell me anything about this. It's mine. I've had it since I was little."

I squeeze the cheap plastic as goose bumps rise along my arms. Warmth sinks through my chest and even though my body's dying, my dad's love swirls through me. I can't forget that. No matter what other news comes along, I hope I never forget anything again. Feeling something, even if it hurts, is better than feeling nothing.

Right now, I need the connection with my dad. He may not have been there throughout my life but he's with me now. I hold the game player in one hand and the statue in the other.

"Thanks, Dad." I keep my eyes on the gifts and the images blur with tears. If I look up, I won't be able to hold them back any longer. It would lead to ugly crying, the kind that makes me cough. The kind that makes me hurt. I hold on tight and Dad touches my hand.

"You're welcome," he says softly. "I love you, Kate. And even though I wasn't there for you in the past, I want to be part of your future."

I press my lips together as a tear drips down my cheek. It's different from the love I have with Mom and it's different from the comforting warmth I get when Kyler's around. And maybe it's not love…yet. Maybe it's just the beginning of something between a father and daughter. Dad and me.

Once he's gone, the waterworks start. Even though I can't see myself, I know it's not pretty, but it's okay because no one's around. Except for Ember, who's already seen me at my worst. She brings me food, helps me calm down, and does therapy with me.

By night, I wish I had someone to talk to again. Ember's putting away my dinner when the hospital phone rings.

Ember answers and tells me, "It's Giana."

I grab the phone and try to hear her through the background noise. "Kate," she says.

"Yes?"

"It was a huge success. I'll swing by in a couple hours."

I check the time. "But that's almost midnight."

"Your dad's right here. He said it would be okay this once."

"Okay. See you then."

I hand the phone to Ember and turn on the game to play electric darts. It's pretty lame, but it passes the time and keeps me grounded in reality. Aim, shoot, score. Over and over. I should go to sleep, get some rest, but I'm too afraid of waking up in a mindless stupor. Maybe after Giana gets here, I'll be able to settle down.

Mom shows up around eleven. "How's my favorite girl?"

I offer a weak smile. "Better."

She holds my hand for a moment then crashes on the couch. "That was some party. I'm not sure how Giana did it, but she got a local band, food vendors, a little train ride, and a ton of other things. It was all last minute too. I ended up teaching karate to a group of kids."

I try to picture the party, but besides Mom doing what she does best, the details don't come easily. "Sounds like fun."

"She was just wrapping up as I left so she should be here soon."

Mom closes her eyes and I tap my fingers on my leg. "Did you know Dad liked darts?"

She rubs her forehead and looks at me. "That's right. He did. I totally forgot."

Her eyes close again and I can see how exhausted she really is. She seems almost as tired as I feel. But I'm determined to stay awake until Giana comes.

Mom's out in no time. I wish I'd thought to ask her about Kyler. Was he there? What was he doing? Did he ask

205

about me or say he'd stop by? Any of those answers would've given me something to think about while I wait for Giana.

The clock ticks on. Eventually it's midnight and Giana still hasn't come. An hour later, I start to worry. She should be here. Ember comes in to check on me and almost forces a sleeping pill down my throat.

I shake my head. "Not yet. Maybe you can dial Giana's number so I can see if she's on her way?"

Ember picks up the phone with an exasperated sigh. It rings four times and Giana's answering machine picks up. Instead of leaving a message, I try again. Maybe she didn't hear it.

She doesn't answer the second time either.

I give the phone back to Ember and clench my teeth. Maybe she fell asleep and didn't have time to call. I glance at Mom and know that's a reasonable possibility. But something doesn't feel right. Not that anything has felt right for a couple weeks, but this is different.

"Mom," I call.

She only stirs.

Ember lets out another sigh and nudges Mom for me.

She bolts up and blinks away the sleep. "What is it?"

"Giana's not here," I say.

"What time is it?"

I swallow. "Almost one thirty."

Mom falls against the couch. "She probably fell asleep. She'll come by in the morning."

Ember puts a sleeping pill in my hand. "You need to get some rest."

I rub my eyes. "I can't. She should be here."

Ember offers a cup of water. "You can call again in the morning. If you don't take this, I might have to add something to your IV instead. And I really don't want to do that."

I take the pill but continue to fight sleep. Giana should be here. I don't think she'd go to bed without calling.

Right before I'm about to sleep, the door opens. I sit up and struggle to keep my eyes open.

"Lie down, Kate," Dad says. His voice is soft and soothing.

I almost drift off, but not until I ask, "What are you doing here so late?" My words slur together and I'm not sure he even knows what I said.

"You need some rest."

"Where's Giana?"

No response. I battle the sleeping pill to stay awake long enough to hear his answer. He has to know. Why else would he be here? My heart beats slower and my body is falling, collapsing with exhaustion. Why isn't he saying anything?

"Giana's been hit by a drunk driver."

Drunk driver.

Drunk driver.

The words echo through my head like an empty cave and my brain shuts off.

Chapter 27

Muffled sounds wake me. I try to open my eyes but they're still heavy with sleep. I focus on the surrounding voices and they become clearer. But they're only whispers. I can't hear definite words. Why are they in my room?

Then I remember.

My eyes fly open and I sit up. My skull pounds, making me lie back down, but now Mom and Dad are beside my bed. Behind them stands a tall lady with dark hair sticking out of a blue isolation gown.

"Kate," Mom says.

"Tell me what happened." I swallow. "Tell me Giana's still alive. I need to hear those words."

Mom nods.

"Those aren't words. Where is she?"

Dad takes my hand and I pull it back. I don't need anything sugar-coated. They don't need to coddle me to deliver the bad news…It'll still be bad. If it were good, they wouldn't look so worried.

"I'll tell you," Dad says. "But I need you to stay calm. After everything that's happened, I'm afraid of what this might do to you."

"Just tell me."

Dad mutters something about me being just like Mom. "Okay," he says. "Giana was hit by a drunk driver. She's in a coma in the ICU."

My head spins and my stomach churns.

"So far, she's been diagnosed with a broken neck."

Paralyzed. He doesn't even have to say it. I take another breath and trap it in my lungs. This *can't* be happening. Not to Giana.

Dad continues. "She's lost so much blood she's in acute renal failure. Her kidneys are beginning to shut down. Other tests are being done right now but that's the worst of it."

Worst is right. No best. I clench my fists and hold back a scream.

"Breathe, honey," Mom says.

I want to do anything but breathe—jab the walls, side-kick the window, tear down everything around me so someone knows what I'm feeling. Dad said it would be okay if Giana came to visit. She's supposed to be *okay.* She's supposed to be prom queen. I open my eyes and find the stranger behind Mom and Dad. Her pale face is streaked with mascara. "Who's that?"

Mom moves to let the lady come forward. "This is Giana's mom, Cindy."

What's she doing in my room? She can't stand to hear Giana talk about me, let alone see me. I don't even know what to say to her.

I face Dad. "Do the docs know how long Giana's going to be in a coma?"

Dad runs a hand down his face. "It could be a day, it could be a month. Really, it's unpredictable."

"What about her kidneys? Can they keep them functioning?"

Dad frowns. "Barely."

Cindy sniffles loudly as she leaves the room.

"Why was she here?" I ask.

Mom holds my hand and I let her. "She wanted to see you. I don't know why exactly, but I'm thinking it has to do with remembering her daughter's courage. Maybe to get a glimpse of her granddaughter's future."

I close my eyes. "That's the last thing she needs right now."

My mind bounces back to Giana and panic rises up my throat. My hands tremble and I can't hold back the tears. What if Giana dies? I've always considered my death, but I've never thought about anyone else's. Death has been staring me in the face my whole life, especially these last few days. Giana might not ever have the chance to say goodbye.

My soft cries turn into hard sobs and I can't get enough air. Mom's trying to calm me down and Dad urges me to take longer breaths.

But I can't—especially now that they're yelling. I'm not even crying anymore, just wheezing and choking and bent in half, coughing up stuff. It comes out red and mom holds my hand tighter as she screams at Dad to do *something*. My throat is on fire and a sharp pain stabs my chest. Dad's racing around me, checking monitors and calling for a nurse. He gives Mom a task, but I lose track of his words. They're just a mix of chaos.

Pain.

Burning.

Dying—

Blackness takes over so I close my eyes and see silver sparkles every time I cough. The pain in my chest shoots to my stomach and shoulders. It's like someone's decided to use me for dart practice. Sharp needles of fire pierce each part of my body and I try to scream through my coughing.

I have to give in. I don't know how to fight anymore.

I pretend the pain is a sad song. Kyler's voice fills my head, but it's not a happy sound. It's hollow, mournful, and it grates at my heart.

I give in to the strange melody and lose myself to the darkness.

Chapter 28

I'm awake. The walls aren't tan anymore. They're white, and they match the bright curtain to my right. At any moment it will open to show me the stairway to heaven. That's where I must be. Why else would my pain be gone?

I try to open my mouth and call out, but the words don't leave my throat. They're stuck on something. I lean my head back and there's a tug from my nose to my stomach. I swallow and it doesn't feel right. This can't be heaven.

I turn my head only to find that I'm still chained to the wall.

The curtain parts and Mom steps through. She comes to my side. "Oh, Kate," she whispers. "My favorite girl."

I blink once and wonder what happened. For the second time in my life, I thought I was dead, but this time waking up is worse. I can't even talk. That's not living, that's being dragged face-down along a rocky road while others get to watch. Maybe if I can get ahold of a cell phone, I could text my words to Mom.

But my hands are bound by needles and tubes. I think this is what they call a living vegetable. Veggies are healthy, though, so it doesn't apply to me. I'm barely living and I'm far from healthy. Can't they just pull the plug?

Mom scoots a chair beside me and sits with her hands in her lap. "You're suffering from respiratory failure."

Medical term for…I should be dead. If they know I'm suffering, why are they making me live this way?

"You're on a mechanical ventilator and there's a tube down your throat. That's why you can't talk."

I try to open my mouth, to prove her wrong, but I can't. I have to think of something else…what else did she just say? More terms I don't know. I'm not sure I even want to figure out what they mean. Mechanical…not my own. She could've just told me I now have robotic organs that can only last so long.

Maybe then I'd actually die.

I close my eyes and try to slip away like I did before. This time, I can't let go of the memories. The wooden carving, Kyler's kiss. Oh, how I want to see him again.

Another voice makes me open my eyes. Dad's standing next to Mom now. His face looks like the one he'd use to deliver bad news to a patient. Maybe I should let him know it's already been done.

"There's still no match for your lungs," he says. "But Dr. Farrow should be here soon."

I want to tell him to stop talking about me, stop telling me things I already know. Isn't there some way to communicate with him? I shake my head and he closes his mouth.

The sudden silence is awkward but it's much better than discussing impossible options. What else would he talk about? Giana's status? I hope she's doing better, but I don't trust my hopes anymore.

"Kyler's coming to visit you today," Mom says. "He told me he'd come by after school, so he should be here soon."

School? I've been unconscious that long? Oh well. Who cares about time anymore? Now that I'm in the ICU, every hour will feel the same. Lights will be on, nurses will talk, patients will make their dying noises. That's why we're all in here, because we're not able to live on our own. I close my eyes and try to take a deep breath, but technically I'm not breathing for myself anymore. The machine cranks out noise and I see my chest rise and fall.

Someone rubs the top of my head before I hear Mom and Dad leave and the curtain pull closed.

It's been a while since I've let my mind linger on Kyler. With everything going on, I feel like I haven't seen him in weeks instead of days. I try to picture his face but I can't remember it perfectly. So I focus on the things I do remember: his single freckle, the bouncy curls, the way my heart leaps when he talks. The moment his lips pressed against mine with a tenderness that set my spirit free. His voice fills my head and I'm walking down a pebbled path. The air is fresh and the architecture is curved, colorful, and unique. A soft violin plays in the distance as a nearby street artist dips his brush into a vibrant blue. The moment is almost perfect, peaceful. If only I could smell baked croissants and not medicines or antiseptics.

Kyler shows up a while later. His space suit *poofs* out the sides as he takes a seat next to me. "Hello, Kate." The simple words send adrenaline through my body. My heart picks up speed and warmth spreads through the cold numbness.

214

Since I can't talk, I nod once and try to smile.

Kyler reaches for my fingers and my chest bursts with a flurry of anticipation. But when he touches me, I don't feel a thing. My happiness sinks and I curse the doctors. Why is my whole body numb?

"The fundraiser went well," Kyler tells me. "Giana had me sing a few songs during the program while they played a slideshow of your life."

I freeze and stare. I didn't know that was going to happen. No one asked my permission for that.

Kyler must sense my unease. "They were good pictures, nothing that showed any of your treatments or anything."

My shoulders relax a little.

"I think it helped people connect with you." He grins. "Trust me, seeing you really helps."

How does it help? I want him to go on, explain what he means. Is it because I look like a little girl so they have more sympathy or is it because he likes the way I look? My face grows hot and I glance at the white walls to help clear my mind.

"Kate."

I turn back.

"I'm sorry about Giana." His eyes are distant. "My mom died the same way. Drunk driver. Idiots. All of them…" His voice trails off, his words weighing me down.

I want to scream, curse, do *something* to release the storm of anger.

Kyler blinks once and rubs his eyes. When his hand falls, the sorrow has melted. He narrows his gaze on me and tilts his head. "When you get out of here, I have somewhere special to take you."

I shake my head. Why do people keep talking about when I get out of here? Can't they see that I'm lying on my death bed? It doesn't get any better than this. There is no more *when*; it's all about *now*.

"Listen," he says.

I keep shaking my head. If he wants to talk about me getting out, he can talk about it with the mortician.

"I got a job," he says.

I pause. I thought he was going to bring up karate lessons or French concerts.

"I'm working at a local French café where I serve food and sing to the customers. It's nothing fantastic, but it keeps me busy."

Busy enough to not think about me and my death. I nod. That's good. It's exactly what he needs.

He sighs and closes his eyes. "And it reminds me of you."

No! No! That's *not* what he needs. Once I'm gone, he can't work at a place that reminds him of the two people who've died in his life. He needs to quit. If only I could move my hands, I'd rip this tube out of my throat and tell him to go away and never think of me again. Instead, the frustration builds inside me and bubbles to the surface. Tears well in my eyes and run over my temples into my ears.

"Hey," Kyler says. "I didn't mean to make you cry."

I blink several times and try to stop the flow of tears.

Kyler's eyes light up. "Did anyone tell you who's on the other side of that curtain?"

The tears stop and I arch my eyebrows with curiosity. He must mean someone besides the cranky nurse that keeps checking on me every hour. Too bad Ember isn't here today.

"Giana's bed is only a few feet away."

I turn my head and stare at the curtain like she might suddenly appear—long hair, healthy skin, happy smile. But that's not what she'd look like now. She's probably tied to a bed with medical devices I can't even name. Just like me.

My gaze switches back to Kyler and he watches me with careful eyes. I wonder what he's thinking. Hopefully he'll quit his job. Once I'm gone, the memories will chase him away from there. Then he'll be searching again for the right song to mend his torn heart—a song that can't be sung to lovers in a restaurant, can't be found in a different language, and probably doesn't even have a name.

But if he doesn't find it, it will find him. He recovered once before and he can do it again.

He hums softly and my meds pull me toward sleep. A content feeling courses through me and my numb body sinks farther into the mattress, closer toward death. There are so many things I'm going to miss, but they can't keep me here. I can't hold onto them any longer. I release the tethered memories and watch them drift away.

No more France. I'll never get to go there in person, and I'll never set foot in a real palace. No more darts or karate. I've finally lost the fight, and there's no more anger to release. No more Giana, no more Dad, and no more Mom.

The only thing left is Kyler. As long as he's singing, I can't let him go. But once he steps past my curtain, my memory of him will also be no more.

217

He hums for a while and when he stops, I'm sure this is the last time I'll see his freckled face. I open my eyes and he's looking past me. I turn my head and find my nurse holding a clipboard with pursed lips.

She pushes down on the top of her pen and it clicks. "Someone informed me that you know a patient here by the name of Giana."

My heart stops. I'm sure of it. Even though the machine still whirs, I try to hold my breath. The nurse is going to tell me that Giana's alive and recovering.

"What is it?" Kyler asks.

The nurse licks her lips. "Her mom wants to talk to you."

My heart skips again and I sink into my pillow. No. *This* isn't the ending I was supposed to have. Why does she want to see me again? I want to pull out the tubes and unplug every machine, but all I can do is shake my head. And I do, over and over. Close my eyes and shake my head like a wind-up toy. Someone cranked my lever and I'm living my last cycle.

Chapter 29

I wish people could read my mind. It would make it a lot easier to request that they move my bed three feet closer to Giana so I can imagine we're in here together. When the noise in the ICU dies down, I pretend to hear her voice on the other side of the curtain.

Ever since Kyler left I've tried to let him go, but the song he hummed is on constant replay in my head. I don't even think I have the tune right, but it's his voice that matters.

I hear footsteps outside my curtain and it opens to Mom, Dad, and Doc Perry standing in a row like they're getting ready to sing me a carol—the solemn smiles on their faces make it seem like a sad Christmas. But I won't be alive for Christmas, so I lift an eyebrow and wait for one of them to talk.

"We have some good news," Dad says.

Maybe they found a donor match. Here I am ready to die and they've found a way for me to live. I try to wrap my brain around the possibility. I can't—it's too much.

They move apart and I see Giana lying in her bed for the first time. So I'm *not* going to live; they didn't really find a donor. *This* is my surprise. And as happy as I am to see Giana lying there, it might've been better for me to die without this image burned in my mind.

This I can't stand.

She's got more tubes in her body than I do, if that's even possible. Her face is bruised and there's a white wrap around her head. And she can't move. Not because of some medication, but because she's paralyzed. Even though I'm numb, my heart aches.

She can't live like this. What kind of life would that be? But she can't die either.

Doc Perry comes to one side of my bed and Dad goes to the other. Suddenly I'm moving closer to Giana. They're putting our beds beside each other just like I wanted. But I'm not sure I want it anymore.

The closer I get to her, the more wounds I see. She has a serious rash across her chin and a deep bruise on her neck. I want to close my eyes, but they stay open. My chest is heavy and my eyes burn with the tears I'm trying to hold back. I can't cry for her like I did before. That kind of reaction might actually kill me this time, and I want one more moment together to make sure there's a chance she'll live.

Our beds are together now with her medical supplies on one side and mine on the other. Someone pulls a curtain around us and I'm left with Giana and her mom.

"Kate," Cindy whispers. Her voice is tired and weak and it rips my heart open.

Even if I could talk, I'm not sure I would. What would I say? I blink out a tear.

Cindy presses her hand to her lips and shakes her head.

I want to tell her I'm sorry or give her a hug...*something*. It's the only thing I can think of. Her daughter is like this because of me. If she hadn't been on her way to visit me in the hospital, none of this would've happened.

"Please," she whispers. "Don't blame yourself. It could've happened anytime."

Another tear falls. Not anytime, not anyone. Giana's already been through a terrible accident in her life. She doesn't deserve this.

"Kate, I have to tell you something." Cindy's voice drifts off and she tries to clear her throat. "Giana's dying."

I barely hear her words. I hope I didn't hear her words. I don't want to hear her words. She takes a shaky breath and I notice that she's falling apart.

"Her insides are shutting down and there's nothing else the doctors can do," Cindy says. "She might only have a few days left to live."

I try to block out her words, but they hit me full force—pressing upon me, cutting off my air. My own death won't reverse time and it won't save someone else. There's no life calculator that says one life can be exchanged for another. I was kidding myself with that thought. We're both going to be dead and that's just the way it is.

I force myself to look at Giana.

"She has one thing left to give you," her mom says. There's a pause and I glance back. She rubs at her frown, but it doesn't disappear. Now her chin's quivering.

What could Giana give me? There's only one thing I need right now and that's... I swallow over and over again, shake my head as hard as I can.

"Yes, I'm offering you her lungs. It's what she would've wanted. They're running tests right now."

I can't stop shaking my head. She wouldn't do this. She wouldn't give her life to save mine. This isn't the cure she promised. It's not even a cure. I'll still die eventually and I can't live knowing there's a part of her in me. My mind scrambles for different options. What was it they said was wrong with her? Her kidneys? That's it. I can give her my kidneys. She can have them when I die and then she can live. But I can't talk; I can't tell her any of this. Cindy's already thought this through and she's a few steps ahead of me. But maybe I'll die first.

"Think of it as a second chance at life," she says.

The only thing I can think of is the end of *Giana's* life. Her lungs won't be a match. They can't. Even if she *is* my size.

"*Please,* don't make this hard, Kate." Her voice is shaky. She sniffles. "Giana didn't want to die. She wanted to be there for her niece. She was so determined to take care of her. Without her, I'm going to need help. I need you to be there. I need to know there's hope, a chance at life. Please take Giana's lungs and take this chance."

I stare at her and let the tears come. They flow into my hair and I force myself to think of her offer not as giving Giana's life for mine, but giving her lungs so I can live her life for her. But I'm nothing like Giana. I'm not nice to anyone and I never reach out for a good cause unless it's *my* cause. I'm selfish and stubborn.

But I can try to change. For Giana, I will. She's giving me something I can never repay. The only way I can show my gratitude is to do my best.

I nod.

Cindy says, "Thank you. You'll never know what this means to me."

She speaks my exact thoughts. She'll never know what she's giving me. Not only is it a second chance at life, it's my *last* chance.

The curtain opens again and Mom comes in with bloodshot eyes. She probably heard everything. I don't know if she's been crying because I might live or because Giana's going to die. Either way, I'm still weighed down. I can't find the joy when one of my only friends is slipping away beside me. Before me. It should be me.

Mom walks over to Cindy and takes her hand. "Thank you," she says. "Thank you, thank you…"

Behind all the medical equipment, Giana's face is peaceful. I imagine her with a smile and capture it in my memory. I'll probably never hear her voice again, never really see her happy. But if her lungs are a match, I will live every day because of her and I will breathe every moment because of what she's giving me.

In her own way, she's found my cure.

She's changed my fate.

Chapter 30

Between nurse checks, therapy, lights on, lights off, and the *whirr* of machines, I never know what time it is. I have no clue if I sleep at night or in the middle of the day. My food enters through one tube and leaves through another. People talk to me but I can't respond. They might as well paint me white and glue me to the wall. I'm useless to them and I'm useless to me.

The only news I hear about Giana comes through the curtain. When I'm awake, I strain my ears to listen for certain signs of how she's doing: soft cries, beeping monitors, and silence. Hearing nothing is almost worse than hearing something. Nothing means she might be gone.

The next time my curtain opens, the trio is back, but with one extra. Dad, Mom, Doc Perry, and a strange man with a scruffy mustache, all in a row. Part of me hopes they'll move to the side so I can see Giana, but another part of me knows they won't. It must be the mix of joy and fear in their faces. They step forward as one and close the curtain behind them.

Silence hangs in the air like a dusty cobweb, ready to trap us if we make a sound. I stare at the ceiling and count the seconds going by.

Before I make it to twenty, Dad says, "We found a match, Kate."

I shake my head and close my eyes. My insides collapse, roll into a knot, and pull me down. I'm falling, silently screaming while I watch each moment with Giana flash before my eyes. They didn't find a match.

A match found me.

Dad clears his throat. "It's perfect, Kate. And it's what her family wants."

No. It's not what they want. They don't have an option. What they really want is for Giana to be alive. They have no other choice. And neither do I. I've told her mom that I'll take them, and I will, but I can't be happy about it. Others may rejoice in my life, but if Giana dies, she breaks the connection between us that I was so hesitant to make. I was trying to protect others, but I never thought I'd have to protect myself instead. Having her lungs in me will never be the same as having her here.

"We'll have to move quickly," Dad says.

Doc Perry responds, "Everything's about ready."

His words stab my heart.

"Which operating room are we in?" the stranger asks.

There's a pause. Each quiet second chisels at my emotions, breaking them apart and scattering them to pieces. I let them go and focus on one thing.

Live for Giana.

Live for Giana.

Live for Giana.

"We're in room three," Doc says.

"Let's get her there," Dad says.

225

Right now? I'm having a lung transplant right now? Is Giana already dead? I can't breathe, can't swallow, can't focus.

Live for Giana.

Live for Giana.

I squeeze my eyes tighter and try to block out the medical words exchanged between Dad and Doc Perry. Even though I can't feel my body, I think they're tugging something—probably changing tubes, pulling some out, putting new ones in, whatever they have to do to move me to O.R. three.

I'm a lab rat again, going through a surgery that will affect an important statistic. If the transplant is a success, I'll give hope to thousands of people with CF. And if it's a flop, it will be studied to avoid future mistakes.

"Is everything in place?" Doc Perry asks.

Someone breathes next to my ear and I flinch. I open my eyes to find Mom leaning over me.

"It's okay, honey," she says.

No, it's not, I want to tell her. We're far from okay.

"You're going to live."

I press my lips together and nod, trying to convince myself she's right. I *am* going to live, but at a cost I can never repay.

"I can't be in the operating room," she says. "But hang on tight and know that I would be there if I could. We're in this together. Stay with me."

I want to tell her I'm trying but there's not much I can do.

The bed starts to move and she steps back, standing in my white cell, wiping her cheek with trembling fingers. As

226

soon as I reach the spot where Giana's bed should be, I search for her, expecting her to be there.

Her bed's empty.

She's already gone.

The thought pounds through my head with a dull thud.

Why didn't anyone tell me? She *can't* be gone. Not yet. Not ever. A sob consumes my throat and I know exactly why they didn't tell me. They knew my reaction might kill me before they could operate. The harder I cry, the quicker they move my bed toward the operating room. We go through a doorway and people in space suits surround me. They touch my head, prick my finger, and switch my IVs. The moment I see the glint of something silver, I shut my eyes.

Live for Giana.

Live for Giana.

Giana is *gone*.

I want to cry more, but my thoughts are being stolen. They slip through my memory and blur together. I grasp for them and try to hold on, but I can't fight the medication. Before I'm completely out, they move me to a hard surface and Dad whispers into my ear.

"Kate. I love you. Remember that. You and your mom have always been on my mind, and I love you both."

His words float in my ear, leave me with some comfort, then drift away.

He touches my hair. "Now go to sleep. Dr. Farrow will take care of you but I'll see you soon."

I hope he does, because I will live for Giana.

I have to.

Chapter 31

The moment my eyes open, I try to take a deep breath but there's still a tube down my throat. My body isn't numb anymore but I can't move my hands. I tug them hard but it's no use: they're bound to the bed. They probably did it to keep me from ripping this dang tube out. I want to take a breath, to fill the lungs that were given to me by someone else. Someone who's gone.

"Kate," Mom says.

I turn my head toward her voice and try to focus on her face. Her image is blurry. I blink several times to clear my vision but it doesn't work. Her voice gives me comfort as I sink into a deep sleep.

The next time I wake up, Dad's standing beside me. My eyes focus enough to see the happiness on his face.

"Hello, Kate."

I try to respond then remember the tube in my throat. Why doesn't he take it out? I reach up and touch it.

He chuckles. "That tube can come out when you start breathing well on your own. You probably hate it, but we need to make sure your new lungs are getting the oxygen they need."

My lungs? He's wrong. They're not mine. I want to correct him...but I can't. I look away and focus on my body. For being alive, I still look like I'm on the brink of death. I'm hooked up to multiple IVs. There's an oxygen reader on my finger, a blood pressure cuff on my arm, several tubes coming out of my chest, and something around my legs that keeps squeezing them.

And now that I'm not numb, I can actually feel some of the pain. Even with all the meds, the skin around my incision burns like it's been stretched too far and might burst back open. Not only does my chest feel like someone's sitting on it, it's also three times larger than normal. Maybe they transplanted more than a set of lungs.

Dad starts talking again, but I'm losing focus. The pillows around me turn to clouds and the bright lights are enveloped by darkness.

I wake up again. This time, Dad's leaning over me with Mom right beside him. "We were just about to take out that ventilator," he says. "It would've been easier with you sleeping, but now that you're awake..."

He doesn't need to finish. Even my slow brain can figure out that this isn't going to be fun. Dad prepares everything and starts pulling the tube from my throat. It scratches and burns and makes me gag.

Once it's out, there's a sharp pain on my tongue. I try to say something, but my throat's on fire. I still can't talk without wanting to kick someone.

"We need you to start moving," Dad says.

"Now?" Mom asks. She took the words right out of my brain.

229

"Yes, now. Nothing strenuous, but the movement will help increase circulation. It will also speed the healing process, clear the lungs, and increase muscle strength. Right now we'll just get her into a chair but later we'll need to go for a short walk."

The anger in Mom's eyes matches the feeling rolling around inside me. They just cut me open like a puzzle and replaced one of my pieces with a new one that might not fit. And now they expect me to move? Have they seen the tubes coming out of my chest?

Dad opens my white curtain and calls to the nurse. Ember comes around, grinning. I'm relieved it's her and not the regular ICU nurse. My happiness dies the moment she makes me sit up.

I gasp for air and cough. Everyone freezes. I cough again and the fire in my throat burns to life. Ember shoves a pillow to my chest and tells me to hug it. I hold on tight and cough once more. Even though the pain is blinding, I can tell the cough is different. It's dry, free of mucus. Still, I swallow and expect something to go back down. But besides the constant pain, there's nothing in my throat. These lungs are clean, healthy. Not mine.

They're *Giana's*.

I close my eyes and force her image from my mind. I can't think of her. Not yet.

"Let's get you into this chair," Ember says.

I lift my eyelids and notice the cushioned chair she's placed beside my bed. Somehow, with the help of everyone in the room, I make it into the chair, where they leave me, in pain, in front of the TV, for two hours. I don't even watch the show, just close my eyes and try to breathe. I think of Kyler, of France, of anything but the pain in my chest and the hard cushion under my butt. Seriously, couldn't they at least put a pillow down first?

The second they return me to my bed, I fall back to sleep.

The rest of my time in the ICU melts together. I'm awake, I'm out. Doc Perry comes, Dad checks on me, Ember's face shows up every once in a while, and I even see the other nurse. It's still hard to focus. When they make me walk, I want to die.

I think of Kyler and do my best not to think of Giana.

That gets harder when they move me to a normal room. My first day there, Giana's mom comes to visit. She doesn't say anything, just sits in a chair, dressed in a space suit with tears streaming down her face. I can't look at her. I won't. I close my eyes and pretend she's not there. As much as I want to help her, I need more time. I'm too broken to help someone else feel whole. Even though I have a part of Giana in me, I'm not her.

But *now* I'm thinking of her. My eyes sting and I smother them with my fists. I need something else in my mind.

Kyler.

Kyler leading me toward the Eiffel Tower.

Kyler singing *La Via En Rose* and giving me soft kisses.

His lips. The freckle.

Anything but Giana.

I hear footsteps and open my eyes. I wipe at the pooling tears to see Cindy walk out the door. Then I inhale

231

and hold the air in her daughter's lungs. She's gone. Giana's gone.

There's another knock at the door. I expect to see Dad come in, but it's Mom.

I exhale and my air rushes out along with all thoughts of Giana.

"How's my favorite girl?" Mom asks.

"Really?" I whisper. "You have to ask?"

Mom smiles. "At least you're talking."

"Trying."

Mom nods and hands me a stack of letters.

I shuffle through them. "What's this?"

"Open one."

I lift the edge of a plain envelope and pull out a blue card with two simple words on the front. *Get well*. I glance at my mom and open it slowly, wondering who it could be from. Inside, I find a short hand written note. "School sucks without you. Get well and come back." It's signed by Vivian and Charlie.

I give Mom a pointed look. "Did you put them up to this?"

She laughs. "No. The office called and asked me to come get them. The students did it all on their own."

I grasp the letters in both hands and my arms tremble. They did this for me?

Mom clears her throat and I tear my gaze from the letters. "It's time for a walk," she says. That's when I notice the extra gown and mask in her hand.

I fall back into the pillows and curse every kind of therapy. Ember comes in and hooks me up to my portable machines. She puts them in a wheelchair and with Mom's help, they get me in my space suit and on my feet. Each step is harder, but one day they'll be easier.

I will get through this: through each day of therapy, treatments, x-rays, bronch checks, and different shots. Each prick and push, pull and shove. They're all worth it. I will make them worth it.

The days continue to blend together and I wonder when Kyler will come. Giana's mom stops by every so often. Each time she cries a little less and each time I'm able to look at her a little more. One day we'll talk. One day we'll share our real feelings in words, but today's not that day.

Today's the day my dad walks in and sits next to me with a hand on my arm. "Kate. You are very lucky to be alive."

I put my fingers on his. It's the first time I've touched him and it feels right. "I wouldn't be alive without you, Dad."

"Sure you would. I'm not even the one who performed the surgery."

I lift an eyebrow.

He shrugs. "I just wanted to tell you why you're lucky to be alive. I've never seen lungs worse than yours."

I swallow. "I was basically dead. Remember?"

"I know. But Dr. Farrow had to break your sternum to get your lungs out. Which is why your movements are so restricted."

"And why I'm in so much pain," I add.

He clears his throat. "I also wanted to let you know that your mom gave permission to send your lungs to the Cystic Fibrosis Foundation so they can research them. Hopefully they can find something that will help others."

I squeeze his hand. "I hope so."

My thoughts go right to Giana. She's the reason I'm alive. Not because of research done on a moldy pair of lungs but because she was lying on her deathbed with the perfect match for me.

"Do you still cough?" Dad asks.

"Not really." I breathe in and let it back out. "It's so weird. I've coughed my whole life."

"And if you don't keep those lungs healthy, you'll cough again. We found an infection in your bronch test this morning and I've upped your medication to fight it off. Let's just hope it's not your body rejecting the lungs."

My skin turns clammy. "Does that happen a lot?"

"Enough that you should be aware of the signs."

He goes through a list of several different symptoms. Basically if I'm sick at all, I'll need to call the hospital.

Dad stands to go. "And once you've done your breathing treatments for about a month, you can probably stop them altogether."

I blink. "Stop? But I've done them my whole life. Won't I still have to fight the mucus?"

"Those lungs don't have CF. You'll still have to protect them from getting infections, but they won't have the mucus build up like yours did."

"Then why do I need to do them now?"

"They're helping your new lungs heal and expand."

Right. *My* lungs. I'm suddenly done with this conversation. Whatever he says. I'll do the treatments, I'll not do the treatments. I'll live each day and I'll do my best. But I'm still not ready to think about Giana. I'm still not ready to admit that her lungs are my lungs...

Dad takes the hint and excuses himself from the room.

234

My next visitor is the one I've been waiting for since I came out of surgery. Kyler comes in with his space suit, the mask hiding his lips and a few curls escaping the cover over his head. Still, I stare at him and a tingle runs up my spine as he moves closer to me.

"Kyler," I whisper.

His eyes light up and he stops beside me. "I knew you'd live."

I nod and swallow. A question enters my mind but I hesitate to ask it. It would mean talking about the one thing I've been running from. But it feels right to ask Kyler. "Did you know Giana was going to give me her lungs?"

He shakes his head and blinks once. "No."

"Tell me…" Deep breaths, rapid heartbeat. "Did they already have a funeral?"

"Yes," he whispers.

I fall apart. Tears stream down my face and I grasp onto him. He leans closer and runs his hand over my arm. He doesn't say a word, just holds me close as I finally mourn the loss of a friend. I couldn't save Giana. I couldn't even make it to her funeral. We weren't friends for long, but it was long enough.

She saved my life.

And she wouldn't want me to live it this way.

I grab a pillow in my free hand and bring it to my chest. Kyler sits on the edge of my bed and wraps his arms around me. I curl in a ball and use him as my shield, protecting me from myself until the grief washes away.

He hums a soft melody and it smoothes the wrinkles in my heart. Giana is gone but there's nothing I can do about it.

I'll think of her every day and I'll take each breath because of her gift.

I lift my head and gaze into Kyler's eyes. They're soft and welcoming and make me want to kiss him so bad. But I can't. I can't risk infection. I push away the urge to tear off his mask and instead lean back until I reach a safe distance. From here, I know it will take more work to get my lips to his. As much as I want it, and as much as it looks like he wants it, it can't happen yet.

"Sorry," I say. "I always cry when you're here."

"It's okay. I cried a lot after my mom passed away. Giana was an amazing person and she made it possible for you to live. We're both lucky to have known her."

"She should've been prom queen," I mumble.

Kyler touches my arm. "Kate." He pauses. "She was."

I tilt my head, on the brink of another breakdown. "That's not funny."

"No. I'm not joking. They kept her in the running and they made her queen."

I don't know what to say. All these kids I've pushed away... I should've given them more credit. I should've been ready to let them into my life. They knew Giana was a good person. She deserved to be queen. Hopefully I can be like her.

"Kyler, when I get out of here, there's something I have to do."

"What is it?" he asks.

"I'll show you when I get out."

His eyebrows shoot up and he must be thinking of the kiss we both want. And even though I want that, there's something else that needs to happen as well. Something that will ease my mind and make each day more bearable.

Chapter 32

A few weeks later, I'm out of the hospital. Mom takes an extended leave from work to be home with me all day, every day. I still have a hard time doing much of anything on my own, but at least I can breathe. Giana's mom comes to visit, and even though we don't talk about Giana, we both know she's the reason there's a connection between us. Cindy asks about CF and we help her understand that it's not just a slow death, but a different way to view life.

When she visits today, she sits at the bar counter and clasps her hands together. "Kate."

I pause, my toast halfway to my mouth. Mom folds her arms and leans against the fridge.

"I have a favor to ask." Cindy's quiet voice is hesitant. "You knew Giana was prom queen, right?"

"Kyler told me." But why is she bringing it up?

"Well...even though they had the dance. They never crowned the royalty. They didn't think it would be appropriate."

I can understand that, but I still don't know where she's going with this.

"I told them the royalty should be crowned," she says. "And I'm wondering if you would stand in her place."

My heart pulses, my knees go weak. "No. Please, I couldn't. Prom was weeks ago."

She puts her hands flat on the counter. "They want to have a special ceremony to remember Giana."

To remember *her*, not me. I have to find a way to get out of this. "But she wasn't there that long."

"*Please*," her voice cracks. "They need closure. And I think it would be good for all of us."

How can I deny her this one thing? I set my toast down and rub my forehead. "When is it?"

"Next week."

Now I *do* sit down. "I'm not sure I'll have enough energy," I say. Really, I'm not sure if I'm ready for all the faces, the sympathy, the sadness. "And what about all those germs?"

Mom comes to my side. "You only need to be there for the crowning. You'll wear a mask and once it's over, you can go home."

I clear my thoughts and make myself agree. "Okay. But only because Giana would do the same for me." Not that I'd ever be prom queen, but she'd stand up there if I was getting a loser award. This is a step in the right direction—to be more like her.

* * *

Somehow I made it through the week. I stand backstage, my hands sweaty and my legs ready to give out. Dad's beside me with my arm linked through his. I lean on him and his forearm flexes, holding me up.

"Just breathe," Dad says.

238

And I do. I inhale through my mask, filling Giana's lungs. This is for her. The prom king is six feet tall, shaggy hair, with a smug smile. I don't even know his name. He glances down at me and I nod.

"Hi. I'm Kate." My voice is muffled but I say it anyway. It's what Giana would do.

"I'm Samuel." His eyes are happy. "You look beautiful, by the way."

Even with a mask on? Dad clears his throat and I mutter a thanks, my cheeks burning. Mom hired someone to fix my hair. Half of it's stacked on top of my head, weaved in braids and knots, with the rest curled over my shoulders. Cindy stopped by and dropped off Giana's prom dress. I stared at it for two hours, not sure if I could really put it on. Somehow I talked myself into thinking it's what Giana would've wanted.

I blink away a tear as the blue sequins sparkle in the backlight.

Samuel steps forward. "It's time."

Our names are announced over the speakers and Dad squeezes my hand. "It will be over in a few minutes. Just try to be happy."

Last time Dad whispered something to me, it was before my surgery. I wondered then if he'd really stick around. Now I'm not sure he'll ever leave us alone. Mom's had to force him out of the house several times within the last couple of weeks. And even though they get along, they're still different people. Whatever they had before can't ever be the same. But I've learned that keeping something the same means that it can't grow. I can't ever be the same; it's time for me to become something different.

Samuel leads me past the black curtains to the center of the stage. I blink through the bright lights and focus on the thumping in my chest. Principal Brown walks towards us with a crown and tiara. His footsteps echo through the auditorium with each *thud*. No one speaks, no one moves. My back is rigid and my hands tremble. The principal places the crown on Samuel's head then holds the tiara in his long fingers. Silence encompasses the room and I close my eyes. I imagine Giana, the queen of a ball. She floats in her blue dress and laughs when they put the tiara on her head.

My eyes burn, but I hold back the tears. Giana would want this to be a happy moment. I look at the crowd and even though they can't see my lips, I smile. Someone sniffles on the front row and I find Mo somewhere near them. His expression is hard, guarded. Another sniffle and a wave of emotion ripples through the room. Giana may not have known the name of each student, but they will never forget hers. Her story will always be alive. And even though she may have only saved my life, her example might lead the way to saving others.

I find Mom and Kyler in the crowd, sitting next to Cindy. The relief on her face is contagious and I finally know the time has come to visit Giana.

* * *

I'm hand in hand with Kyler and he's leading me to the place I know I need to be, but am hesitant to get to. We walk through the grass and a warm breeze floats across my skin. The air smells of plants, flowers, and life, but the surrounding headstones are solemn beacons of death. Each step toward Giana's grave seems to weigh me down. I'm still not sure what to feel. I've thought of this day over and over again. But

240

now that it's here, my mind's in limbo. I've grieved over the loss of a good friend and celebrated the new life she's given me. And even though our personal connection is gone, I still think of her as being with me all the time.

Kyler stops and points to a grave on my right. I'd been so lost in my thoughts, I didn't see it coming. The black lettering stands out against the pearly white marble. I stare at the words and remember the first time I saw Giana, handing me the food that saved my day. And now she has given me much more. Below her name and living years is a quote. I whisper it softly. "Always giving—"

I close my mouth and hold onto the words. The sentence lingers in the air, waiting to be finished. But I can't say it, it's too real and it's too much.

"Even in death," Kyler says, finishing the quote and hugging me close.

I clench his shirt in one fist and the stem of a rose in the other. The thorns prick my skin and remind me why I'm here. I take a deep breath and fill Giana's lungs with air. Even though she lies beneath the ground, part of her is still alive.

I kneel beside her grave, place the red rose beneath the quote, and rest my hand on top. As much as I'd like to speak the words running through my mind, I can't get them to come out. I sniff back a few tears and feel Kyler's hand on my shoulder. He knows what I want to say and since no one else can hear me, I say it to myself.

I'll never forget you, Giana. You've given me a lifetime of breaths. You're selfless and caring and never once hesitated to call me friend. I'll be there for your family and give your niece all the hope I can. No matter how much hope that is, though, it can never match the amount you've already

241

given me. With your lungs, you proved that you could change my fate. As long as I live, there will be a live rose on your grave, representing your life that continues in me. I'm forever grateful. I'll miss you, Giana, but you'll always be with me.

I press my hand against the cool stone and stand. Kyler leads me to the car without a sound. Before opening my door, he pulls me close. His arms tighten around me and his minty breath lightly touches my face. His gaze is piercing, his eyes singing songs that only my heart can hear. He whispers something in French and kisses me softly on the lips.

I'm flying free, soaring across the sea, dancing around the Eiffel Tower. My heart flutters a million beats, reminding me that I'm alive. Alive and not alone.

Too soon, the kiss ends and we get in the car to drive away. And even though we leave Giana behind, she'll be with me forever. Without her, I couldn't have this moment. This breath. This life. I didn't know what it meant to *be*, but now that I do…I can finally *become*.

Thank you for purchasing this book.
You have *be*come part of the cause to finding a cure.
To learn more about cystic fibrosis, visit www.CFF.org.

Acknowledgments

I'd like to thank God for being with me on this journey every single step of the way. This book was supposed to be written and apparently I was supposed to write it. Thanks to my parents, who taught me what's most important in life. My hubby, for his constant support and endless love. My little princesses, who make me smile every day. Jamie and Regan, who inspired this whole thing and who also introduced me to Sara. I could have never written this book without you, Sara. You taught me about CF and brought this idea to life. Tiffany, who is my personal cheerleader and cover designer. Janie and Nina for their willingness to jump on board and capture the meaning of this book through a lens. My editor, Alice M. for your countless hours on getting everything just right. TK Productions (Kindra) for the awesome headshots and book trailer. Your skills are magical! Thanks to Shallee, Melanie, Carol, Annette, Kelley, and my many beta readers who caught little things to make the story shine. You're all rockin' awesome!

Most of all I want to thank my college roommate, who offered her book exchange money to assist my small family still in school. My neighbor, who helped me get three little kids to a third floor apartment on a regular basis. To my friend, who brought a carload of groceries in my moment of struggle. To the countless people in my life who've taught me what it means to *be*. Hopefully, together, we can all *become*.

About the Author

Michelle Merrill loves kissing her hubby, snuggling her kids, eating candy, reading books, and writing first drafts. She names her computers after favorite fictional characters and fictional characters after favorite names. To learn more about her, visit www.authormichellemerrill.com.

53842323R10152

Made in the USA
Lexington, KY
22 July 2016